LIGHTING
THE
WORLD

Also by Merle Drown

The Suburbs of Heaven

Plowing Up a Snake

LIGHTING
THE
WORLD

Merle Drown

Whitepoint Press
San Pedro, California

A Whitepoint Press First Edition 2015
Cover and book design by Monique Carbajal

ISBN - 13: 978-0-9898971-4-3
ISBN - 10: 0989897141

Library of Congress Control Number: 2014951574

Published by Whitepoint Press
whitepointpress.com

For my three sons
Jim, Matt, and Devin

LIGHTING
THE
WORLD

Heard from a distance the boom and crack of gunshots can be surprisingly muffled. Because the halls of Rumford High School had recently been carpeted and the stairwells equipped with sound deadening material, the building absorbed the roar of exploding shells; at its farthest reaches, the library and cafeteria, all noise disappeared. The puzzled students kept in those areas heard nothing. Those locked in classrooms close to the shooting still did not know what had happened. Even those who saw it could not say why.

Rumford, New Hampshire
Late Fall 1985

Doing Good
in the World

"No man's luck holds," Wade's father said at supper after he had explained that Uncle Andrew's girlfriend had left him. She had lived at Andrew's trailer in Vermont and had taken care of him, but she had gone off with a man whose legs worked.

When Wade picked up the phone, his mother asked whom he was calling.

"Uncle Andrew."

She grabbed the phone right out of his hand and slammed it down. "You're not running up my telephone bill calling that druggy uncle of yours."

Wade cursed himself for not lying when she'd asked whom he was calling. "I'll pay for the call."

"If you have money banging around loose in your pants, you can contribute more of your pay than the fifty percent you turn over now. It's time you found out that life isn't all handouts."

He was finding out what life was, faster than she wanted him to. In the morning he dug the Xmas card list out of her closet and wrote to Uncle Andrew asking him if he needed help.

In the kitchen the grease-filled pan from his mother's bacon sat on the stove like a pool of stagnant water. Jelly doughnuts, bacon, coffee, and cigarettes—Velma Rule's daily breakfast—stunk up the room. Wade was amazed that fat didn't drip from the walls. He was more amazed that she stayed slender, the same one hundred thirty-five pounds as Wade, nearly the same five foot eight. Every morning she left the kitchen for him to clean: skillet, cup, plate with bacon grease, doughnut crumbs, and ashes left like the remains of a kill. In the woods the rotten smell of dead meat sunk into the earth, escaped into the sky until it disappeared naturally. In this apartment all her smells stayed until he cleaned them, scraping carcasses into the garbage, soaking the dishes in the hot sudsy water, scrubbing the skillet with steel wool.

"I told Rich you'd be a great dishwasher," his mother had said when she got him the job at Big Rich's. "It's what you do best at home."

The restaurant work had softened his hands, then toughened them, so that now, cleaning his mother's mess, they neither stung nor burned.

His stomach turned over. It felt stuffed, full up, as his father said this morning. "I feel so stuffed that if I ate anything it would come right back up." At forty-five, Frank Rule, though still strong for a medium-built man, had a sloppy beer gut, and blue eyes that peered weakly from under the thinning light brown hair that hung over his forehead.

"Your eyes are so pale," Velma Rule told her husband,

"that I can see right through them. And don't you forget that." Velma herself had dark eyes no one could see through. Wade didn't like to look at them, thatched as they were by heavy eyebrows like wooly bears.

That night his mother gave Wade hell for going through her belongings without her permission.

"Here," he said and laid a dollar on the table to pay for the stamp.

"Your uncle's a druggie which is why his girlfriend left him," his mother said. "He was a drunk, and now he's a druggie. Is that what you want to be?"

Uncle Andrew took pain pills for his injuries, and whose fault was that? But Wade didn't bring it up to his mother because she'd made up her mind about Uncle Andrew. He didn't tell her that he was saving his money so he could take himself to Vermont where he would tend to Uncle Andrew and hunt all he wanted. He snickered when his mother pocketed the dollar. That's all her principles amounted to. One dollar and no change.

"I've got my standards," she said. "He's a hypocrite, him and his religion." Her thick eyebrows crinkled, and her thin nose scrunched up as she lit her Salem and claimed her dollar's worth of standards. "You needn't laugh, Wade Rule. I've done my best to keep you away from drugs. As long as Andy is a druggie he won't step foot in my house, and I won't step foot in his. And that's that."

You wouldn't spend the money for the gas, Wade

thought.

"Andy's always looking for a handout," his mother said, "and that's that."

At sixteen he had discovered that all the good things in life disappear.

Maria

About the same time as Wade decided to live with Uncle Andrew, Maria started waitressing at Big Rich's. On their break while Wade drank a Coke and she poured herself a coffee, he told her he planned to leave his house. Almost immediately he felt she was both trustworthy and sympathetic.

She stirred in one carefully measured spoonful of sugar. He noticed right away that she was accurate, neat. Uncle Andrew would say she was a together woman, her dark hair in place, her clothes pressed, even the books in her knapsack orderly. "I need to move, too," she said.

"Maybe we can help each other," he said.

"I'd like that, Wade," she told him, her thin lips spreading into a smile. "I really would." Her face always moved quickly, precisely, whether to smile or to frown.

Though he'd barely known her a day, that smile told Wade she liked him. He'd had romantic feelings before, even for Ms. Plizak, his biology teacher last year, but this was love. This revealed a Wade Rule even he hadn't experienced before, as genuine as the Wade who'd hunted back in Newfound or hugged Uncle Andrew's back as they'd sped on the motorcycle. This was so real that Wade knew if he felt it, Maria must feel it too. She didn't have to say it because it was in her smile. In fact, he didn't think he wanted her to say it, not yet.

"I'm going to Vermont to take care of my uncle," he told her.

"I love Vermont."

That was all she needed to say.

The next time they talked she said she wanted to tell him about her father. Wade asked her if she smoked. "Because if you do, I'll get cigarettes for you," he said. "Just tell me which brand."

He didn't like smoking. His mother flicked her ashes carelessly all over the house, risking burning the place down with Wade and his father in it. He had decided his mother didn't care if he lived or died, but he knew if Maria smoked, she'd be neat about it.

Maria reached across the table and patted his arm. "No, but that's sweet of you to offer. You don't smoke, do you?"

He shook his head and sipped his Coke and told himself to shut up so that he could listen to Maria tell him about her father. After all, she wouldn't like him very long if he didn't listen to her. And how would he ever learn anything about her if he didn't let her talk? He wouldn't pretend to read minds, like his mother, he knew that for sure.

Maria didn't have a mother. A lot of kids didn't have fathers or at least not fathers who lived with them, but he didn't know anyone without a mother. He was about to tell

Maria she was lucky when he remembered not to interrupt her.

Her mother was dead.

"It was when I was in grade school," Maria said, "but I remember it."

Wade said he hated how when you said something happened when you were little, your mother would say you were still young.

"Sometimes I feel I've never been young," Maria said.

When Maria lifted her cup, he saw there was no spilled coffee lying in the saucer, the sloppy remains his mother always dabbed with her cup bottom, then dribbled on her blouse. All her uniforms looked like some careless child's finger-paintings.

"Maybe that's a silly thing to say," Maria said.

"It's not silly," Wade said.

"Maybe it's just melodramatic."

But what she told him about her father crashed past melodrama. The man cursed her, berated her, fouled the very house with insults and insane demands. When she studied, he called her a bitch, a whore. Man was given dominion over the beasts of the field, Uncle Andrew used to say, he wasn't supposed to become one. Maria was going to leave her father. She was a smart girl, having already looked into the legalities of leaving and still keeping the social security money she received because her mother was dead.

Wade hadn't heard from Uncle Andrew. He hoped for a letter inviting him to move to Vermont right away, a letter with directions because Wade didn't know exactly where Uncle Andrew's trailer was. Somewhere near Brattleboro, his father had told him, but not in a trailer park. His father had said it took eight windy roads to get there and ten windy roads to get back. Wade didn't care how many roads it took to come back. Maybe Uncle Andrew would call him.

"When I leave, I'm not letting anybody talk me out of it," Maria said. "No one will stop me."

"Me, too," Wade said. He finished his Coke and held it like a hand grenade he could toss at all their enemies. "No brag, no bull, just go."

"Will your father help you?" Maria asked.

"My father's one big disappointment."

He told Maria how last year in tenth grade his father had taken him ice fishing on Lake Winnipesaukee. All week Wade had waited to go. He'd looked forward to riding up through Newfound, where he used to live, because he might see his old friend Ernie.

"Cold," he told Maria. Cold, starting at fingers and toes, had crept through every cell of his body. Even his butt had frozen, hunkered so close to the ice while he waited for the flag to dip. His father had brought only one chair, which he sat on.

They had luck, catching three good-sized lakers, but

his father forgot the fish and the bucket beside the car and drove off without them because he drank nearly half of a fifth of hard stuff, "anti-freeze," he called it, making him tired.

In the car Wade said, "I would've liked the fish for supper." Wade was thinking of frying the fish with a little cornmeal. He didn't say a word when his father cuffed him. He watched his father's eyes dipping, and Wade worried about him falling asleep.

"What are you staring at?" his father yelled. Then he backhanded Wade. Wade stuck his nose in his book for the rest of the ride. When they pulled up in front of the house, his father didn't say anything, and Wade didn't say anything. Then his father punched him in the mouth.

"But he was too worn out to really hurt me," Wade told Maria.

Maria said his father had committed child abuse and should be turned in to The Division of Child and Youth Services.

"Does your father ever hit you?" he asked.

"If my father hit me," she said, "I would report him to DCYS. It would get me out of my house easier than what I'm going through now. But he doesn't touch me, neither a slap nor a hug. He doesn't want to lose the survivor's benefit money."

Wade said he forgave his father. "That's a better way. My uncle used to say if you can't be the light at least bear witness to it."

It was the same story he'd told Ms. Plizak, but that was last year when it actually happened. He felt cheap using the same story with Maria after he'd already told it to Ms. Plizak, not that either of them would ever find out. Though nobody knew much of anything about Wade, he wanted to keep himself honest, not false.

Ms. Plizak had sat tall on her high stool behind the long black-topped biology lab bench, while he sat in one of the student desks in her room, where they ate lunch together once or twice a week. She would make gentle fun of the peanut butter-cheese crackers he munched on, the junk food he bought across the street at Cumberland's. He could tell sweet teasing from stupid teasing, like ninth graders calling you "zit face." He had known Ms. Plizak's sweet teasing meant she liked him.

She said all her teaching about nutrition was going to waste and how junk wouldn't make him a hunk, but he had known she worried that he couldn't afford a better lunch. So that Friday he'd brought four packages of crackers for her and, as a joke, a blueberry yogurt.

"You're a blueberry kind of woman," he told her. He chose blueberry because he remembered a summer day spent picking blueberries with Uncle Andrew on a high slope that faced the lake in Newfound. Afterwards his mother had made blueberry pie. That day had stuck in his mind, all the sweet-smelling sunshine he'd tasted in the chock-full, blueberry pie.

"A luncheon date," Ms. Plizak said, "and he buys."

Wade knew calling it a date was another kind of teasing, to make sure he didn't feel uncomfortable. It wasn't a date, though Miss Plizak was pretty, the prettiest teacher at school. In the bio classroom on Monday Wade pulled down his lower lip to show Ms. Plizak the cut from where his father had punched him.

He didn't want Ms. Plizak feeling sorry for him. One day he could take care of the old man himself. He'd read about hunting accidents where people died alone in the woods. Wade could wait. He'd waited for that damn fishing trip like a kid waiting for Christmas. No more. His father was no Santa Claus, and fishing with him was no holiday. His father had betrayed Wade like a cold wind in May. One day he'd like to see that the old man felt the cold whistling through his backbone.

The third time he shared a break with Maria, Wade waited until his mother finished her shift and left. She left by the restaurant's back door. She never used the front door. Not only was the front door of their apartment locked, an ugly divan blocked it like a fat, passed-out drunk. In Newfound too she had used the back door.

His father claimed to use whichever door he pleased, but in Rumford he used the side door without a whimper.

Not a whimper, Wade thought, after his mother had said she wouldn't change things around just so his father could traipse in and out of two different doors.

"I'm saving up money to go to Vermont," Wade told Maria. They sat facing each other in a booth, she rearranging her hot fudge sundae, he cradling a Coke between his small hands.

"How much do you have?" Maria asked. Her attention to details showed again. Actually Wade had just started saving. If he held back the half of his pay that his mother demanded, he'd have seventy-five dollars.

"I hate my mother." He would tell this only to Maria. He wondered if she knew that.

"She's nice to me." Maria dipped her spoon into the top of the ice cream to get a precise portion. No slop spilled from her spoon. "Does she bug you about school?"

"She doesn't try," Wade said. He swigged some Coke and banged the can on the table. "I can see my mother cut up into pieces." He'd never told this to anybody. If they were real smart, they'd figure it out. Maybe there wasn't anybody that smart in the whole world.

"You're always reading a book," Maria said. "You're too smart to want to hurt somebody."

"I only do what I want to do."

"I have to see a lawyer," Maria said. She jammed a syrupy gob between her teeth. Fudge oozed over her chin. "Oh, damn."

"I don't need to stuff and mount report cards on the refrigerator so's my mother'll be happy."

He'd said enough about his mother, but Maria kept talking about her. Ice cream and fudge slipped into her mouth, but some lingered on her lips. Maria said his mother had helped her when she started working at the restaurant, showing her how to write out a check quickly, how to fill a sugar bowl as she cleared the dishes from a table so that by evening's end the place would be ready for the morning shift, even how to give back money so the customer would have change for a tip.

Wade congratulated himself for putting Maria at ease. "Tell me where you live," he said. As she talked, he drew a diagram on an open napkin. He linked street to street and sketched trees at intersections and set shrubs around her apartment building. It stood way past the North End, in a poor section called The Mills. Finished drawing, he folded the napkin, map side in, and with it blotted away the syrup from her chin. "There," he said, showing her the chocolate splotch, "now I'll be sure to keep it." He tucked the napkin into his shirt pocket.

First Date

If Wade had a car, he could drive Maria home after work and to school in the morning. He could even load all her things in the trunk and drive her to Vermont. Uncle Andrew's trailer had three bedrooms, which meant one bedroom for Uncle Andrew, one for Maria, and one for Wade.

Car, hell, he didn't even have a license.

Sometimes he saw Maria at school, but mostly he saw her at work. The work itself, running dishes through the washer and scrubbing out the pots, he didn't mind, the hot steam soothing his brain and sometimes reminding him of misty mornings in the woods.

Whenever Velma Rule came into the kitchen, she'd tell Wade to work faster or ask how many glasses he'd broken or pick a skillet off the clean pile and run a nail over the surface to lift any grease. "Rich," she'd say to the boss, "you find Wade slacking, you let me know. I can't afford for him to lose this job."

Rich always said that Wade was a good worker.

Wade longed to see Maria outside the restaurant or school, on a date, but he needed a ride to her place. Riley had a beater, a gray-primered Dodge Dart. Although Wade knew the car would never see real paint, he didn't care what it looked like just as long as it got him to Maria's. If things worked out, he'd get Riley to drive them to Vermont.

Riley said, "It runs better than it looks, and it'll look better when I get done with it."

It wouldn't. Wade knew that cars like Riley's beater took all your money in repairs so you never got to dressing them up. Riley, like most people, would talk about doing things until the time to do them had passed. Death and junk always caught up with you, caught up with you unawares. He agreed with his mother about that.

On Wednesday Wade sat with Riley on the tippy wooden bench in the high school smoking area with the fall sun beating bright and hot in the asphalt valley outside the cafeteria. Wade shifted his weight to rock the bench. "Just like 'the twister' in *Lord of the Flies*," he said.

"What?" Riley asked. He squinted and squeezed the filter tip of his cigarette as if he held a joint. Riley always had to act tough though Wade thought he was a good enough guy.

"In this book where these kids got stranded on an island start hunting one another," Wade explained. "Little kids sit on a log and call it the 'twister' because—"

"I read it." Riley leaned back. "Just couldn't hear you. You mumble all the time for Christ's sake. I had to read that goddamn book for English last year."

Wade had read the book because he'd wanted to read it, but he wouldn't tell Riley that, any more than he'd tell

Riley how much the high school resembled that fictional island with its big kids and little kids and cliques. "Think I could get a ride with you to The Mills?" he asked Riley.

"The Mills?" Riley said. "Why d'you think I'd be going to The fucking Mills?"

"I heard you say you were going back where you used to live, up past The Mills to Boscawen."

"Barnstead. I used to live in Barnstead."

Maybe Riley, too, mumbled because Wade was sure he'd said Boscawen. Wade had registered it and told himself, Maria lives on the way to Boscawen. Wade knew people would hear him if they cared enough to listen to what he said.

"I'll give you gas money," Wade told Riley. "Fill your tank."

"I got nothing else to do tonight," Riley said. "What do you want to go to The Mills for?"

"Girl."

"Yeah." Riley scuffed his cigarette under his heel. "Funny how you never find a girl in your own neighborhood. I'll bet there's guys from The Mills coming to your neighborhood to see their girls."

Wade had not expected Riley to say anything this close to philosophical. "One more game we got to play," Wade said. He held no hopes Riley would continue the conversation though he had offered him a half-idea. He was glad Riley didn't wise off about Maria, but then Riley wasn't into teasing.

Although under Riley's uniform of regular was an inside pocket of good, Wade wished for more than just good. He wished Riley had an interest in learning why games like dating always led you off someplace else. He wanted to use words to track ideas, like hunting down reality, goodness, the light of the world. Riley wanted to talk about where they were going to meet. The good in Riley lay in his not being bad—a dull, neutral kind of good.

When Riley'd moved to Rumford last year, he hadn't had any trouble with kids calling him funny names. Unlike Wade, he'd moved in free and clear. In ninth grade some kids called Wade "Chipmunk" because in class he'd said he liked to hunt. Hell, Wade didn't even shoot chipmunks. Most of these Rumford kids had never fired a gun, to say nothing of killing prey; they couldn't imagine what a shotgun blast would leave of a chipmunk, fur and blood. Wade's long, fluffy hair reminded some other kids of pioneers, so they had called him Daniel Boone.

Uncle Andrew, remarking on Wade's smooth cheeks and halo-like hair, had said he looked like an angel in a Renaissance painting. Uncle Andrew also called him Rumpty-De-Dump, which Wade didn't mind because it was Uncle Andrew being funny, though it was even stranger than angel. Strange from Uncle Andrew was a compliment.

Rumford didn't take kindly to what it considered

strange, and though Riley was a stranger to town, he ran a long way from strange. Riley had a straight, regular-sized nose, straight, brown hair, stood five ten, and could probably lift his own weight. Wade would give Riley the regular award. He was the most regular guy Wade knew.

Though no regular guy would be called "Chipmunk," it didn't mean anything, just small game that Wade passed up. Put these kids in the middle of the woods, even with a gun, they wouldn't know what to do. They'd die in the woods unless someone came along to help them. They'd shoot a chipmunk then be shocked because there wouldn't be as much as a single mouthful left. If guys like Riley got lost in the woods, Wade would save them, but guys like Riley didn't venture into the woods.

That afternoon Riley met him at the pizza parlor. That was Wade's idea because his mother was working late at the restaurant. He set the pizza box on the seat like an offering to the great god Riley.

"Don't they give you a discount at your job?" Riley asked.

"I don't eat where I work," Wade told him. He said it clearly enough so that Riley couldn't accuse him of mumbling. It wasn't a major principle of his philosophy, though he hoped Riley might ask him a question, just to start a conversation.

Wade knew Riley would want his promised gas, so he

wasn't surprised when Riley pulled up to the self-serve pumps at Pik-Quik and sat behind the wheel. I've got to buy it and pump it too, Wade thought; just like my mother, Riley likes somebody to wait on him. Makes them feel like royalty. We live in a democracy, and people want to be kings and queens.

As the gas rushed into the tank, Wade figured Riley had another motive; he wanted to see if Wade really would fill his nearly empty tank. Wade kept his hand closed on the cold pump handle. The kaleidoscopic digits ran to ten, eleven, twelve, and past thirteen dollars when the back pressure burped the pump off. He eased in a few tenths more to round it off at $13.50.

"Hey, Wade," Riley said. He handed a ten out the window. "The Mills ain't that far."

Wade ignored Riley's money, paid for the gas, and bought some Coke and chips too. When he tucked himself into the front seat, the paper bag in his lap, Riley asked him, "Hey, dude, did you get us some beer?"

"Munchies," Wade told him. "Maria doesn't drink beer."

"Cranking tunes and eating pizza, great life, huh?" Riley said. Riley didn't eat pizza; he wolfed it, two pieces to every one of Wade's. Riley bit a healthy halfway into the narrow end, chomped that down, folded the rest and crammed it into his maw.

Wade liked that word "maw," which he had discovered

in horror books. Monsters used their maws to mutilate people, stuffing their maws with the foolish and the innocent. When he'd first seen the word, Wade had thought it was a misspelling for "Ma," "Mother," maybe written in a way to make you pronounce "Ma" in baby talk, but that meaning had made no sense in the horror books sentences. The dictionary in the school library had told him what "maw" meant. Still, he liked his original ideas. Ma— Mother mawing up the foolish and the innocent, taking them into her gullet, grinding them with crushing stomach muscles, dissolving them in the digestive acids of her huge dark cavity. Riley mawed another yellow and red pizza piece like a slice of flesh. Wade laughed.

"What's so funny?" Riley asked.

"Nothing," Wade said. Riley was too regular a guy to understand it.

Listening to Riley drive away from Maria's place, Wade felt lost. He looked up at the brick building and wondered how many apartments it held, lined up on each of three floors, down hallways. He wondered which one was hers. That was stupid. He'd drawn this great map to find Maria's address, leaving out how to find Maria herself. Some hunter he was.

Checking the entrance to locate her name on one of the mailboxes, he realized he didn't know her last name. There were twenty-four apartments in the building. He'd have to knock on each door and like a dork say he was looking for Maria I-don't-know-her-last name. If he could carry a gun to hunt in the woods, he could screw his courage up to walk through this building. It would be easier if he had a gun because then people might take him seriously. Inside the entryway Maria met him.

"Four o'clock," she said. "You're right on time."

"I knew you'd like that," he told her. "Which apartment is yours?" She pointed to the mailbox labeled Blanchard #14, and he promised himself he'd write it down on the napkin-map.

They walked outside where the sky had started to darken. Maria said her place was a mess, her stepmother was fussing over some awful stuff on the stove, and her father was home. They walked up a hill to a clearing with a picnic table, a memorial park to somebody. Wade started feeling his courage.

"I have a record," Wade said, and as he glanced at Maria to see her reaction, the garlic taste of the pizza he'd eaten in Riley's car haunted his mouth. Maria put her hand on his shoulder.

"Did you bring it?" she asked.

"What?"

"The record." She pointed to the bag he gripped close to him to keep the food from slipping out.

"A jail record." Hadn't he said that? He knew he hadn't mumbled. "I got us Coke and chips in here." He held up the bag.

Above the row of pines that edged the park, the sunset died in waves of red. For a moment he waited for Maria to speak. He felt irredeemably foolish. "Back in Newfound the police gave me a record," he said. The sunset would have made better conversation. He should have talked about the sunset.

"Did you do it?" Maria asked. He looked down as she grabbed his hand and pulled him to her side of the picnic table. "Sit here where you can see the sunset."

"They always get you for something."

A small smile crossed Maria's face. She was the nicest girl Wade had ever known. He sat beside her, letting his thigh touch hers, his shoulder lean against hers.

"What did you do?" she asked.

"Dealing fireworks." He told her the cops caught him because a naive friend let off some fireworks right in town, not a hundred feet from the cop station. "I didn't care. You get caught; you get caught." He gritted his teeth. Just like Riley, trying to sound tough. He stared off into the darkness that had settled at the base of the pines. The fizz of the Coke made him aware he'd opened the two liter bottle. Maria ripped the bag of chips and passed him a handful. "But the cops made a big deal to get our supplier. Ernie was ready to crack. You know what the cops do to try to scare you?"

Maria shook her head. She was a good listener. She was about the only one who listened to him at all, so he tried to make his story accurate.

"They put you in separate cells to scare you into ratting on your friends. They were going to use their nightsticks on us." He wouldn't talk about Slim Jim's reputation with the nightstick because that was too dirty to tell Maria. His leg tightened uncomfortably, but he didn't want to move and lose contact with her. She bent to grab more chips. When she leaned back, she shifted so that their bodies no longer touched. He handed her the Coke and watched her tilt it back to her mouth. He noticed she didn't wipe the bottle top before she drank.

"They didn't know Ernie's brother was the one who got us the brick of firecrackers," Wade said. "They might as well have tried to talk us into killing ourselves as ratting on him." He laughed, nudged Maria with his elbow, and left his elbow against her arm. She laughed too and handed him back the Coke, moving away just enough to break the touch. "Ernie knew I was a true friend. He knew I wouldn't rat on his brother."

"Did you have to pay a fine or something?" Maria asked.

Wade spread his hands as if he were unveiling a painting. "Those Newfound cops. They took what was left of our firecrackers and put me on probation."

"I thought you were the dealer."

The unattended Coke bottle slipped, spilling cold liquid between his legs. He clutched it before Maria noticed.

"They had me down on the ground with a gun to my head, and I said nothing. I know what it is to be a true friend."

He reached into the chip bag and pulled out two big ones. He hated the little chips because they slipped between his fingers making him dig for them in his crotch. His crotch was already wet with Coke.

Maria pushed her fingers through his hair, lifting it away from his face and fluffing it back. He closed his eyes. Her fingers soothed him. "You're no juvenile delinquent," she said. "You're too smart for that." She stopped brushing his hair, and he opened his eyes. "Give me some more Coke, please."

"You know what I was thinking?" he asked. "When you open a brick of firecrackers, the red tissue paper they're wrapped in crinkles, and then you get an almost wet, stone smell of the gunpowder when you open one of the packs. It leaves a shiny, silver-gray dust on your fingers."

"Can you still get fireworks?" Maria asked. "I really like the pretty ones."

"I have a catalogue," Wade said. "It's from Pennsylvania. Or Ohio. I forget which. They sell some beauties. Skyrockets, fountains. Displays they call them. But you can't get M-80s. Nobody sells M-80s anymore."

He'd liked the catalogue. Filled with pictures of pyrotechnics, as they called fireworks; it showed all sorts of packages, just like you were ordering from Sears, only Wade had never had money to order. He told Maria he'd bring her the catalogue, then he remembered his mother had thrown it out when they'd moved from Newfound. "I'm not dragging a lot of useless clutter," she'd said, "and that's that."

"I hope to leave in the next two weeks," Maria said. "My father is a criminal."

Oh, God, did Wade feel stupid, bringing up about his record to impress her. He might just as well have worn a shirt that said CRIMINAL and stuck his signed confession on her refrigerator. "What did he do?" The sun sunk closer to darkness, leaving only the pale, gray light along the horizon. If he were hunting, it would be time to get out of the woods.

"You know, Wade, I haven't told anyone at school about this." She took his hand and held it between hers as if she were praying, with his fingers as an offering. She squeezed them so tight it hurt. "He committed arson, but he did it in Manchester, which is why no one up here knows about it. I'm going to court to get away from him before he has his trial." She let go of his hand, lifted the Coke, and slugged down a big swallow. "He's not a pyromaniac or anything psychological. He just did it for money."

Then he told her about Uncle Andrew in Vermont, about moving there to take care of him, about the spare bedrooms in the trailer. Their plans wove in and out of hope and anger, dodging any dreams of desire for each other. He sensed that without asking. It wasn't cowardice that kept him from asking but sense, his own good sense that Maria liked him, trusted him, and would wait for physical love.

Maria had to see a lawyer and go to court to get free of her father. Wade had to turn criminal to free himself. A couple of miles off to the south the state prison lights lighted the sky with a dull glow even as the western horizon went black.

"West," he said, pointing. "That's where I'm headed, west to Vermont."

"I envy your independence," Maria said. She fumbled with her fingers. It was the first time he'd seen her make an uncertain move, as if she suddenly found herself unsure about something. "I don't even know where I'm going. My father says he'll have me put away. I could get sent off to some foster home. I know I'll run off to Vermont or anywhere before I'll live with Steven Blanchard any longer."

Next week was her appointment with the lawyer. Wade needed to hurry. If he didn't get a letter from Uncle Andrew, he'd call him, even if he had to use a pay phone. Riley could easily take Wade and Maria to Vermont. Wade knew Maria liked him and knew she would quickly see how a simple ride to Vermont could free them and solve both their problems.

"How are you getting home?" she asked.

"I'll bum," he said. He knew she was getting ready to

go into her house.

She stood and stared west toward Vermont. "There aren't many cars on a weeknight. Do you want to call your parents?"

Maybe, once in her apartment, he could stay for a while. She'd get him a glass for his Coke. But he'd have to make the call home, and that he wasn't going to do. His mother didn't give a care where he was, and his father would be too far into his beer to notice he wasn't home. Maria probably wouldn't let him stay very long anyway because she had homework to finish. What was he going to do, call home to say he was leaving, then stay with Maria for another hour?

She walked him to the road and patted his shoulder. "Thanks for the munchies," she said.

He handed her the bag with the chips and the Coke. "You keep it. But be careful. I couldn't find the bottle cap."

Cat-and-Dog
Fight

He walked five miles and never got a ride. It was nearly ten when he turned his key in the lock. The house was dark, his parents asleep. He had a vision they'd die in their sleep. In the morning he would have to cut up their bodies like dressing out a deer, fit the pieces into garbage bags, and get rid of the whole mess so the police would not blame him for their deaths. Then, he'd live on his own without having to lie. Though he believed "the truth shall make you free," living with his parents made it hard not to lie.

How much had he lied to Maria about Slim Jim? Four or five years fade details, the scent grows faint, you lose the trail. Still, he tried to remember, remember accurately, even if it were five years ago.

The half pack of fused together firecrackers sounded like gunshots. "I got an eight-shooter," Wade said.

Ernie said, "You ain't no Western dude."

Ernie threw his half pack, but only four crackers went off. Wade searched through the grass for the duds.

"What'd you want those for?" Ernie asked.

Ernie had put up most of the money for the half brick of firecrackers they'd bought. Wade had wheedled two bucks from his father. "It ain't Fourth of July," the old man had said. "It's September. What are you celebrating, the start of junior high?" Then he'd slipped Wade the money to buy the firecrackers.

Ernie had given his older brother eight bucks, along with Wade's two, as easily as if he were paying for a Coke. Nothing stingy about Ernie, he shared the firecrackers fifty-fifty with Wade. Showing Ernie how to light duds would give Wade a chance to make it equal between them.

"You need pavement," Wade said. Uncle Andrew had shown him how to do cat-and-dog fights.

"You're making this up, this cat-and-dog fight bullshit," Ernie said. Ernie, skinny and no taller than Wade, could argue with his words without threatening with his body. It was just the opposite of Wade's mother. Wade had asked for movie money, and she had slapped his face: argument, answer, and judgment all in one.

"Come on to the old school grounds, and I'll show you," Wade challenged him.

They left the field at the end of the railroad tracks to walk to the playground where the elementary school had burned. "So many kids hated this place," Ernie said. "It burned just from their thinking about it."

"It was brick, wasn't it?" Wade could barely remember the old school. "How could it burn?"

"My brother said you pile enough books and papers together, you can burn anything. Enough bullshit, you got to show me this cat-and-dog trick or eat your words. Hey, did I tell you I saved your reputation the other day? This kid said you ate shit sandwiches, and I told him he was a liar. Told him you didn't like bread."

Wade bent one of the dud firecrackers in the middle until he could see the black powder start to spill from the split in the layers of paper. He set it on the tar. The flame from his lighter caught the powder, which hissed and spat and spun the firecracker around.

Wade could tell Ernie really liked it when he grabbed for one of the duds to try it himself. Wade would show him one more trick. Quickly, Wade crimped another dud to expose the gunpowder. As soon as it started to burn, he stood and stomped it with his boot heel. Blam! He swore it exploded louder than the crackers that blew up the regular way.

"Jesus Christ," Ernie said. "Give me one of those."

The first one he missed, hopping around as if his pants were on fire. But the second one he stomped right on time. After a third, Ernie wanted to compare a whole firecracker with a cat-and-dog to see which cracked better. He tore open a new pack, the red tissue paper blowing across the lot only to stick against the chain fence. Ernie told Wade not to turn around so they could do a scientific test.

Along the bottom of the fence that Wade faced lay dirty papers, ripped chip bags, old cigarette and candy wrappers. Sun and rain had dulled their colors until they took on the gray of cat puke. Wade thought one day it'd all be gone, just like the school. The whole thing—tattered papers, cracked asphalt, even the town, a dud with no one to light it.

Blam! Then a few seconds later, Blam!

"Which was louder?" Ernie said.

Wade tried to decide if he should guess which was the cat-and-dog fight. He knew Ernie wanted that one to be the louder one.

Fingers locked on Wade's flesh between his neck and collarbone. A quick pain tilted his head. He looked up at the six foot six cop they called Slim Jim. Slim Jim flung Wade to the ground. From there the cop treed above him, a dark pine with powerful limbs out of nightmares. Slim Jim was the youngest and meanest cop on the Newfound force. He put his hand on the butt of his gun and ordered Ernie to turn over all the fireworks.

Slim Jim grabbed the bag of firecrackers from Ernie. "This is all official evidence." He pushed Ernie down next to Wade. "Both of you better eat dirt or you'll get a slug up your butt."

Wade worried that Slim Jim would search his house where he had several more packs. Then he began to worry that the cop might actually shoot. Slim Jim could always say that they were trying to escape. Wade could feel his bladder trying to let go.

"Saving up kind of early, ain't ya?" Ernie said to Slim Jim. "The Fourth of July ain't for another ten months."

Wade, neck still aching from Slim Jim's grab, turned his head to look at the cop. In one hand Slim Jim held their dozen packs of firecrackers, the black cat arching his back on the top pack's flimsy red paper. The other hand hovered above his weapon, as if Slim Jim himself were the Western Dude, just waiting for Wade or Ernie to draw on him. If Wade moved wrong, Slim Jim would shoot him. Wade wanted Ernie to shut up.

Wade had heard that Slim Jim beat up guys in the station, really tamed them. Ernie's brother said Slim Jim searched some guy for drugs, made him strip naked right there in the cell and stuck his nightstick up the guy's ass.

"All right, you little delinquents," Slim Jim ordered, "down to the station."

Slim Jim didn't have to handcuff them because his hand on his hip kept them from running. Running? Wade wished he could creep, crawl, do anything to delay entering the station. Crossing the hill humiliated Wade. At least two of his classmates saw him and Ernie, a couple of captured sheep Slim Jim herded toward the station. He could hear their questions, first day of school. "How far up did he stick his nightstick? Was it just his nightstick?"

On the opposite side of Central Street was City Hall, a red brick building that gaped at Wade. He wanted to look at Ernie, but he feared Ernie would say something that would get them hit. Or shot. The entrance to the police station jutted into the side street that ran along the building. POLICE, the overhead sign said. They would pass under it and down into the basement, the cellar, the bowels of the building. It was going to hurt. Wade's neck still hurt, though not enough to make him hold it. He wouldn't show Slim Jim that he was hurt. Tired muscles clenched his groin, squeezing shut his bladder. He hadn't pissed his pants. He wouldn't piss his pants.

Slim Jim made him and Ernie sit at opposite ends of a ten foot long table. At a desk against the wall Slim Jim rolled a long form in a typewriter and, faster than any secretary Wade'd seen, made the machine fly over the paper. He snapped it out smartly then laid it in a black plastic tray.

Strong fingers gripped Wade's neck and hoisted him out of his chair. The earlier pain returned. With a jerk forward, he tried to escape, but Slim Jim pushed and held so that Wade stumbled, the tight pain still burrowing in his skin.

"Move!" Slim Jim ordered.

Now beside Ernie, Wade backed his head out of Slim Jim's grasp. He was free. He looked at Ernie, and pain behind his knees crumpled Wade to the floor.

"Wrong, peckerhead," Slim Jim said. He stepped on Wade's fingers. "Just stay on the floor while I'm talking. You don't deserve a chair."

Wade glanced up at Ernie; Ernie did not grin. Their luck hadn't held. It didn't really matter what they did or didn't do. Slim Jim had them.

"You got a record now," Slim Jim said. "You guys would fuck up a wet dream." He said he'd busted them because anybody stupid enough to shoot off firecrackers in broad daylight in the middle of a playground could turn dangerous. They had no common sense.

Grabbing Wade and Ernie by their arms, Slim Jim shoved them down a corridor to the holding area where he locked them in separate cells. He asked them where they got the fireworks. Sitting on the mattress slung from the wall, Wade knew he wouldn't rat on Ernie's brother, but now Slim Jim would beat them up. Or worse. He wished Ernie would tell.

"Your brother, right?" Slim Jim told Ernie. "He's worked up a real fine record, your brother. Selling firecrackers to kids would be nothing to him." Slim Jim slipped his nightstick out of his belt and dragged it across the cell bars, thrusting into the space between each pair of bars as he went. "I know it's your brother, but I'm going to hear it from your mouth before I'm done."

Back across the bars came the stick, all the way to Wade's cell, smack-thrust, smack-thrust, smack-thrust. "You, too," Slim Jim said. He left the nightstick protruding into the cell while he stared with angry dark eyes that condemned Wade to hurt.

Hurt ran black from Wade's neck to his bowels; Wade wouldn't tell. He felt his thighs jumping, jumping.

"We found them," Ernie said. "We found those firecrackers by the railroad tracks. Finders keepers, losers weepers."

That sounded good, Wade thought, a good lie, especially the part about the railroad tracks. "This morning," Wade said.

Slim Jim dragged the stick across the bars without poking it inside the cells, just banging it from bar to bar until he reached the door. He said, "I'll be back." Sliding the stick back into his belt, he smiled a greasy smile that knotted Wade's guts, then left.

"I won't tell," Wade said to Ernie. His legs had stopped jumping. He stood and grabbed the bars between his cell and Ernie's.

Ernie pointed up. "Keep quiet."

"I told you I would," Wade said.

Ernie pointed to the surveillance camera sweeping its lens over the cell area. Wade figured it had a microphone.

"He'll let us sweat here awhile," Ernie whispered to Wade. "He's hoping we'll let something slip."

"I'm not going to say anything," Wade whispered back.

The air in the holding cells was hot and dead. Even just sitting on the mattress, Wade sweated. The mattress smelled. Lysol or some disinfectant, he thought. Maybe guys pissed on it. Or something else. No, not with that camera. Maybe. Maybe they rolled on their sides and did it with their backs to the camera. He got off the mattress and paced. He had to pee, but he wasn't going to pee in front of that camera.

"Quit that pacing," Ernie said.

Wade slid to Ernie's side of the cell and whispered, "Because they'll think I'm hiding something?"

"Because you're making me nuts," Ernie said.

A long while later Slim Jim came back, dragging his nightstick across the bars. "Like it here? Want to spend the night?"

Wade looked to Ernie for help. He wanted Ernie to tell because it was his brother. Wade wanted to tell, but he wouldn't.

"Hey, Rule!" Slim Jim said. "Lighten up." The cop, like his mother, could read his mind, his fear. "I'm releasing you to your parents. Keep your noses clean."

That was it; that was all; they were free to go. Only when his mother talked to him that night did he know Slim Jim hadn't done him any favors.

"He's trying to help you," Velma Rule said.

"He swore at us," Wade told her.

His mother ignored the accusation. "I don't know about Ernie, but his older brother's got stripes printed all over him."

Puffy about the eyes, Wade's mother talked slowly, as if she were ill. Slim Jim had said something to hurt her. He wished she would bawl him out. He wished Slim Jim had punched him or hit him with his nightstick. Then he could plan how to get back at Slim Jim and redeem himself, instead of sitting in the living room chair and feeling like a piece of dried dog dung so pitiful you wouldn't even kick it out of the way.

At home from Maria's he tried to shake that rot from his soul. Wade's slant-ceilinged, narrow rectangle of a room held no stuffed animals, no paint-faded Hot Wheels, no squirt guns from long-ago water wars, no furniture other than the single bed. Nor were relics of his growing up stored in the attic. His mother had saved nothing when they'd moved from Newfound.

"Clutter and junk," she'd said. "There's no room in my life for junk, and that's that." Wade's room held his few clothes, books, a water-stained poster of *The Shining* that his rich friend Peter had given him, and his shotgun.

Wade tried to remember the exact first loss. He liked to be accurate, as accurate as he was when he hunted. At school he wasn't accurate because school accuracy didn't matter, except in math. Even in math exactness only meant numbers. He figured it had all started to go bad three years ago when Velma Rule had moved Wade and his father from Newfound with its seven or eight thousand people to Rumford which was five times bigger and a lot richer, though their apartment, chopped out of an old house, looked like their apartment in Newfound.

Living in Rumford would cut twenty minutes driving

time for his father, who worked at Rumford Ford road testing cars the mechanics repaired. "He drives all day," Wade's mother said. "He shouldn't have any extra driving to do."

She hated living in Newfound, where Frank's former sister-in-law tried to steal Frank from her. The ex-sister-in-law spread lies saying Velma had stolen Frank from his first wife and threatened her. She caused a row in the restaurant where Velma worked, which cost Velma her job.

"She's trying to kill me," Velma said.

"She's not trying to kill you," Frank told her.

"I don't work, I don't eat. I don't eat, I die."

Velma said that living in Rumford would make it easier for her to visit her mother, an Alzheimer's patient in a county nursing home near Manchester. "Here in Newfound I see more of your ex-in-laws than I get to see of my own mother," Velma told Frank.

"You could stop working and take care of your mother," Frank said.

"Yes, and how long before you'd be running off to that ex-sister-in-law of yours to whine about how miserable you have it? Aren't we near to eating dirt with me working?"

Wade knew living in Rumford was going to be bad the first time he talked to John, a friendly neighbor kid in his eighth grade gym class. "Where do you hunt?" he asked John.

"I don't," John said. "Where do you?"

"Anywhere there's woods."

"There are woods in Rumford."

Helpful, John tried always to be helpful. Still, he hadn't understood that Rumford was a city where you couldn't just take your shotgun and walk out the backyard to shoot, not on South State Street, where John and Wade lived. You probably couldn't even carry a gun without the police stopping you. John had lived here all his life, so he couldn't understand walking up your road to hunt. Knowing he had the skill and power to shoot a deer gave Wade a joy he couldn't explain to John, for whom four or five trees together made a forest. Maybe it was enough that John had understood that Wade missed Newfound. It was more than anyone else in Rumford understood.

The rich kids at school called Wade's clothes "blue light specials" as if he shopped at K-Mart. These rich kids didn't know he didn't shop at all. "Sticks and stones may break my bones," his mother said. "Tell that to those smart ass, rich kids."

Wade wondered how many lines of foolish wisdom had been preached to him. Don't take handouts, his mother always said, don't give hand-ups. But she gave him advice all the time and was always willing to teach a new waitress or put in an extra half hour at work. "Keep your nose clean," Slim Jim told him. My nose is clean, Wade thought, as clean as the barrel of my shotgun.

He wished John had a car because he liked John more

than he liked Riley. John wouldn't even ask him why he had to drive to Vermont. Right now they would be in the car driving, and Wade would be telling him as naturally as eating pie why he was taking Maria to Vermont.

Back in ninth grade, John, a little taller than Wade and a good thirty pounds heavier, played JV football, wearing his blue and white uniform with all the pride Wade felt in hunting. He asked Wade to play football too, even just a pick-up game in the play-lot up the street.

"No way," Wade told him. Wade knew football. It wouldn't be just John playing. It would be other guys too, bigger guys who liked to throw their weight around and pick on smaller guys.

Wade played basketball with John, but only if there was no contact and only if there weren't many guys playing. HORSE—he liked to play HORSE. Shooting baskets was like hunting. You stood in one place, aimed, and let go. Then you watched the ball arc through the air at the target. He wasn't great at HORSE, he wasn't even good at it, but making weird shots or laughing at John clowning with wild hooks or alley-oops made him feel good. He knew why HORSE reminded him of hunting. No one jostled you or bumped into you or grabbed you when you shot HORSE. And accuracy always counted.

When John bounce-passed Wade the ball, he always put top spin on it so that it shot off the asphalt at Wade. At first he'd thought John was trying to make him miss the ball. Then John had shown him how to twist his hands to give the ball speed and still place it where he wanted. John had explained how you wanted to give the opponents little time to steal the ball. Wade belonged to no team, but John just naturally wanted to show people how to do things, and he hoped he was smart enough to go to college so he could teach little kids. Wade just wanted a cabin somewhere to read and fish and hunt. Wade's father liked to hunt and fish, but he lost his patience after he gave in to Wade's mother and moved to Rumford. He lost his soul, and Wade knew that once you've lost something, the only way you could fix yourself was to move on your own and find something else.

The Way
to Die

Going after his first deer four years ago in Newfound, Wade carried his father's shotgun broken. The shells stuck brass end up from his bandolier. It was early Saturday morning, and all along Pleasant Street no one made any noise. A light mist softened the shapes of houses and trees, only the brass rounds gleaming brightly. He had to walk just a mile up the hill before he could cut into the field bordered by woods that sloped all the way down to the Winnipesaukee River. He knew there would be deer bedded down in the field. He also knew that by the time the sun warmed the white frost from the weeds, the deer would disappear into the woods. All but one, the one he would have shot.

The night before, his father had promised to take him hunting. As usual on the second half of the rack of beer, he had called Wade "Bob," the son from his ex-wife. "She hit the Oregon Trail," his father had mumbled, "so my kids wouldn't have to lay eyes on me again."

He had taken the last bottle with him when he'd left to pick up Wade's mother. She was working late at the restaurant to make extra money. "Give her a treat," his father had said. "Squire her to the Vets Club." That was okay. His mother deserved that.

On the floor the six-pack carrier had lain like a small

wounded animal. Wade had tucked it into the wastebasket, then tucked himself into bed. His father wouldn't poke a foot out of bed before dawn. Sometimes his father kept his promises. Sometimes he didn't. Wade was just sorry his father wouldn't see him shoot his first deer.

Pleasant Street was pale white without a hint of yellow. The street lights still showed faintly in the false dawn. Shades and blinds hid the insides of houses. Wade was twelve years old, by law not old enough to hunt deer alone. His twelve-year-old face, with neither whiskers nor zits, would fool no one into thinking him older, but he didn't worry. He felt as natural as the morning mist. Who in Newfound would care? He carried the shotgun broken and empty. He threatened no one. He started no fires like the one that had burned the school. If someone heard Wade's shot, he'd think some man got lucky this fine November day. It was in season, and Wade was using a shotgun, as was required within the city limits, silly as it was to think of Newfound as a city. Who could complain? Just because he didn't have his father with him?

Once he had stepped into the field, Wade slid shells into the gun and snapped it closed. He released the safety, then reset it. The sun, showing from just below the hill, told him he was nearly a half hour into the legal hunting day. No wind blew his scent to the deer. He told himself he was lucky. He hoped there was a buck, a big buck with a rack on him. Could his luck hold that far? His father had told him some men wait years and years to get a deer and then, it's so small it looks as if they bagged some farmer's German shepherd. Other men, like his father, got their deer the first time, a deer to feed a family for four or five days. His father had tilted back the bottle of beer, leaving Wade to guess which sort of man his father thought he'd be.

Wade stopped. He dared go no farther. From here he could hit anything fleeing into the woods. Although it would be surer to tramp another half mile up the road then cut back through the woods to get behind the deer, by then they might have scattered. He stood still, watching the sun. Red streaks flowed across the sky, tinting the landscape until Wade thought he was standing in a field of quiet blood.

In the beautiful light two deer, does fat with fall feeding, rose where the herd bedded. Their nostrils quivering in the cold air, they turned toward each other, then to him. He didn't move. They didn't see him. Then they did. They could see him no matter how good his luck was, no matter how much he didn't move. With a bound they leaped toward different parts of the woods, their white flags held high. Wade heard them crash among the trees. He pressed the gun to his shoulder and kept his hand wrapped around the stock. In the east a tinge of yellow appeared. Wade would wait for the buck.

A skipper, this year's fawn, leaped up and dashed to the

wood. Just behind him ran another doe. Still Wade waited. The sun showed true red now. Maybe he had waited too long. He raised his face from the gun. His eye looked to the field with no barrel to sight along. He stepped forward. The frozen wild grasses crunched under his boots as if he walked over bones. White under his feet—white clear across the field, all the way to where the buck stood.

He ran toward Wade, toward the road. Almost as soon as his eyes found the barrel, Wade squeezed a shot, then another. The buck, antlers high enough to catch the sun's red, kept running. Wade pumped another shell into the chamber. Before he could fire, the buck fell.

When he reached the deer, Wade knew he'd suffered buck fever. Only once, only that one instant. Not in aiming, not in squeezing off two slugs, but in dropping his gun to run through the melting frost to the buck. He was lucky the gun had not gone off and blasted a hole in his back as neat as the one he'd made in the buck's chest. The first shot, too high on the neck, drained blood. The buck didn't quiver. That was the way to die, sudden, quick, complete. Wade ran back for his shotgun. Why was he running? The gun wasn't going anywhere. But he ran all the way, picked it up, and ran again, this time to the edge of the woods where he would drag his buck.

Dragging the animal was far harder than he'd thought. At his first pull, his boots skidded on the slippery grass, spilling him backwards. He laughed. Nothing could spoil this time. Grabbing the antlers, he swung the buck sideways and, hunched over, walked backward, the momentum helping him to slide the animal. The buck must have weighed two hundred pounds. Again Wade slipped. He decided he had moved far enough from the road. With the hunting knife from his belt, he field-dressed the buck just as his father and Uncle Andrew had taught him. Yanking handfuls of grass, Wade covered the buck. The sun, now high enough to have lost its colors, shone on the yellow field. Wade broke the shotgun and headed for home to wake his father with the news.

"What are you traipsing home now for?" his mother said when he got there.

"Traipse," she said when they moved to Rumford. "I'm not going to traipse down to the city with that deer head of yours. Rumford people have pretensions of civilization. Besides, that thing gives me the creeps, staring at me like I was the one who shot it."

"Uncle Andrew paid two hundred fifty dollars to have it stuffed," Wade said.

"So give it to Andy," his mother told him. "He needs something to watch him all the time."

Although he knew she was being sarcastic, Wade gave the trophy to Uncle Andrew to keep at his trailer in Vermont. Uncle Andrew told Wade he mounted it right on the living room wall. He knew what it meant to Wade.

When Wade moved in with Uncle Andrew, there would be his deer head to welcome him and to make him feel at home.

Uncle Andrew

Wade called his father's youngest brother "Uncle Andrew," though everybody else in the family, including his mother, just called him "Andy."

"Andy's funny, all right," Wade's mother told his father, "but it's not funny the next morning when I'm cleaning up the mess."

She said that even though Andy was twenty years younger than Wade's father, they both thought they were better than she was. "Arrogant, that's what they are," she said.

Why she called them arrogant, Wade couldn't understand. Velma Rule herself acted arrogant the night she threw Uncle Andrew out.

Uncle Andrew had ridden over to Wade's house on a black and purple Kawasaki Ninja. "This cycle goes so fast it'll scare the fear right out of you," he said.

But he gave Wade a smooth ride, goosing the bike up hills and leaning it through curves on the lake road, exciting Wade with the thrills of floating with speed. Uncle Andrew balanced the bike so accurately Wade could squeeze his knees against the smooth black seat, lightly grip his uncle's back, and let himself zip through the streaming air.

On the way back from the lake, his uncle rode to Wade's

friend Ernie's house. He sounded the horn and brought the Ninja to a rumbling, panting stop in the driveway. Ernie stared at the machine and thumped Wade's helmet, but he refused the ride Uncle Andrew offered. Wade didn't tease him because Ernie couldn't know how absolutely safe and accurately Uncle Andrew rode the purple Ninja.

"Andy could ride that bike through a waterfall and come out dry on the other end," his father said.

Later that night it rained. When Uncle Andrew went outside to tuck the bike next to the car in the garage, he'd walked limber-limbed from all the beer and liquor he'd drunk with Wade's father. An hour later the two of them started singing loudly, slow songs from the fifties, the harmonies jamming sourly into the corners of all the rooms. Wade, unwilling to go to bed, fell asleep on the living room couch with the old melodies playing in his ears. Splintering wood woke him.

"Every time Andy's here, this is what happens!" His mother punctuated her yelling by beating his father with the broken chair rung. "You two destroy things I can't afford to replace."

"We were only been funning," Wade's father said.

She swung the chair rung like a sickle over the table, flinging smashed glass to the four walls.

"Out, you!" she yelled at Uncle Andrew. "Get on your damned old motorcycle and ride out of here!" She threw the chair rung, catching him full in the face, then grabbed up another stick of chair.

"You can't make him leave after all he's had to drink," Wade's father said.

"I didn't make him drink," she said. "I didn't make either one of you drink."

"Momma," Wade said. "It's pouring outside."

"I didn't make it rain either," his mother answered.

Uncle Andrew held his face. Blood slid between his fingers from his nose or mouth or eyes. Wade thought Uncle Andrew could see out of only one eye. "Okay, Velma," Uncle Andrew said, "I don't want to cause trouble."

Wade heard the Ninja's roar, then heard it whine up through the gears. He used to think he had actually heard the skid as the tire broke away from the road, though Uncle Andrew had been more than a mile away. In soft roadside sand, the front wheel had hit a chunk of tar, like stubbing your toe, Wade's father explained afterwards, and somersaulted Uncle Andrew into a telephone pole, which he'd hit upside down and backwards.

Days he lay in intensive care, so hurt Wade hadn't been allowed to see him. When they moved him to a room, Uncle Andrew in a giant white cast showed only a little flesh, puffed in black bruises. Wade didn't speak. He cried for his adventurous uncle who would never ride a motorcycle again.

"You wouldn't think a man had that many bones to break," Wade's father said.

Uncle Andrew had broken his back.

After a month, the hospital sent him to a rehabilitation center in Vermont, but they didn't rehabilitate him. They taught him to use a wheelchair. Afterwards, he settled in a trailer with a woman who worked at the center. Wade said it was awful what happened to Uncle Andrew.

"He's lucky," Wade's mother said. "He lived through it, didn't he?"

The
Accidental
Son

Thursday morning after his date with Maria, instead of waking to the heavy grease and smoke smell, Wade woke to Velma Rule's voice, sharp as an X-Acto knife, cutting through the walls of his room.

"We had this out over that daughter of yours last year," she told his father. "That was that."

"She's pregnant, Velma," his father said.

"You think I work all day so you can send money to an able-bodied girl sitting on her butt in Oregon? If your ex had taught the girl right, she wouldn't have gotten pregnant when she couldn't afford it."

Though his mother kept calling her a girl, Stephanie was in her twenties. Wade listened to hear how much his father had sent. Mostly his mother slashed his father with the promise he'd made not to send money after those kids turned eighteen. "I won't be strapped by that brood, Frank. Didn't their aunt tried to steal you from me? Didn't I lose my job in Newfound through that woman's evil? They'd walk right over me if I needed help, so I can't see how anyone would expect me to take the food out of my mouth for them. Just how stupid do you think I am? It was plain insulting to short me from your paycheck and then lie about how that money had gone to a new retirement plan!"

One time Wade's father had shown Wade pictures of his "other family," two girls and a boy, all with long brownish hair, sitting outside with trees and a trailer in the background. In one of the pictures they were standing on a beach, which Wade realized was the Pacific Ocean. One day he could drive Uncle Andrew, along with Maria, to visit this other family and see the Pacific Ocean.

Fifty dollars, his father had sent fifty dollars, which his mother repeated as if she'd discovered his father had taken up with his ex-sister-in-law. "Fifty dollars! And a promise to send her fifty dollars every week. What did you think, she'd name the baby after you?"

"You had an accident once," his father said. Wade wished they'd stop arguing so he could go out there.

"My accident was in trusting you to take precautions," his mother said, her voice low and grindy. "I told you as long as you were sending money off to those other brats, we couldn't afford any kids. And you agreed. Back then I didn't know you were a liar and a fool. That was my mistake, thinking Frank Rule knew enough to wear a condom."

"All right," his father said. A mouthful of soggy cereal softened his word. "So we had an accident. I don't see—"

"You don't take care of him. Do you know where he went last night? Or what he did? Wade!" she shouted. "Wade, get up!"

He, Wade, was their accident. Good, that suited him just fine. They hadn't wanted him. He didn't want them. He wished he'd known it earlier. An accident, it must have been dark, really dark, for both of them.

"Wade!"

His name blasted out of her mouth at full choke. If he didn't show up in the kitchen in a hurry, she'd rush in and strip the bedclothes off him, as if to catch him whacking off.

"You owe me thirty-eight dollars," she said as he slid into a kitchen chair. "Where is it?"

Every week she took half his pay, leaving him the rest to buy lunches, clothes, and anything else he needed. He was supposed to feel lucky because she took all his father's pay and doled out five dollar bills for him to buy beer.

"I haven't cashed my check yet," he said.

"Too busy rushing off God knows where yesterday to give it to me to cash," she said. "Or don't you trust your mother with it?"

His father started to say something, but without looking she waved a bony finger for him to keep still. She wanted an answer from Wade.

He felt his finger start to jump, move on its own in spite of his trying to make it look like meaningless drumming on the table. Covering it with his left hand, he told her he forgot.

"You didn't forget to ask Rich for it."

Grabbing him under the arms, she hoisted him from the chair, spun him halfway around, and snatched his wallet from his back pocket. There it was, money left from the paycheck, less what he'd spent on gas, chips, and pizza. She said something sarcastic about dishwashers hoarding tips, then the X-Acto knife came out again. She was tired of being cheated and lied to while she worked six days a week, took care of the house, kept the finances, and tried her best to see that this family of Rules didn't wind up in jail or on welfare, like all the other Rules had.

"You two drive me crazy with all your conniving. When I'm in the nut house, we'll see how you'll fare. You wouldn't bend your knees the right way if God had given you a choice."

Taking all the bills from Wade's wallet, ten more than the thirty-eight dollars she said he owed her, she sat down and drew on her cigarette as if to give her strength. Wade thought she was going to cry. He remembered when his father had kept the checkbook, the sheriff had come to their Newfound apartment with an eviction notice; his mother had cried. Since then she had paid the bills. His finger stopped twitching. He reached for her.

"And where were you last night?" she asked, as she peeled the ash from her cigarette. "Bothering Maria, I'll guess."

"I went to her house," Wade said.

"That girl has enough problems without you bothering

her." Now the voice turned instructional, as if giving directions for a test. "You stay away from her. Maria doesn't need to wind up pregnant. We can't afford any accidents."

Wade wondered if she knew he'd heard them arguing. Then he announced he planned to quit school. His mother dragged deep on her cigarette, pursing her narrow lips, and creasing her cheeks. He felt her sucking the air out of him. She told him to go ahead, then he could work full-time and contribute a full share to the household expenses. He didn't tell her he wouldn't be part of her household expenses anymore because he'd be living in Vermont. He doubted his mother was serious, telling him to quit school, because she turned quickly from him to his father, who was leaving.

"See if you can wrangle some overtime," she said. "Maybe you can send your knocked-up daughter money out of that."

Even when she's kind, she's mean, Wade thought, as if goodness scared her.

To prove his own truthfulness, the first thing Wade did at school was to ask for the Withdrawal From School Form in the guidance department. While Mac, his first period social studies teacher, talked about the Friday test, Wade studied the form. It was very simple. So simple, in fact, it made him wonder if maybe they'd given him only part of the form. A single white sheet asked for date and name of student at the top. Then he saw the catch:

My son/daughter is withdrawing from school this date _____ *with my knowledge and permission for*_____*(reason for withdrawal)* _____ *(signature of parent/guardian)*

Thinking up a reason to satisfy that blank line would be easy, but what about the signature? His mother might stand in his way, especially if she figured out he was going to Uncle Andrew's.

Below the dreaded signature of parent/guardian line stood two ranks of lines labeled *Subject* and *Teacher*. Did he need permission from all his teachers to quit school? They often told him he didn't do as well as he could. Whenever he hadn't finished his homework or worked hard on a paper, he would feel he had let down the teacher, especially if it were Mac or Mr. B, someone he liked. Shame and embarrassment weighted his head, making his neck bend.

He could tell his teachers he was moving to Vermont. That wasn't really a lie. He'd leave out that he'd be working full-time there to support himself and Maria. Maybe they'd have a night school there where he could study for his G.E.D. He wanted to finish high school, even if it wouldn't help him live in the woods and hunt and fish. He wasn't stupid. To earn enough money to buy land and lumber for his place, he would need a better job than washing dishes, some job that required a high school diploma.

At the bottom of the signatures column were the

directions: *To be initialed by subject teacher/librarian when student who is withdrawing has returned all books and materials.* Wade could forge initials. He didn't owe the library anything because even though he read in there, he didn't borrow their books. His class books he'd leave in his locker so they could find them. He was no thief. He'd sign his mother's name. He would spare her one more thing to do for her accidental son.

His friend Peter, sitting beside him, took notes with an erasable pen as fast as Mac chalked stuff on the board. When Wade asked to borrow the pen, Peter whipped out another, brand new, and handed it to him. He didn't like fooling with the pen, which he had to twist and erase to make his writing come out halfway decent. A pen was not his tool. With a gun you didn't fool around. They didn't make erasable bullets.

Hunting was not a game like John's football or an entertainment like the movies Peter loved. Hunting was real, life and death in your hands, not like school where you competed for pretend goals to train you for adult life, when you would pretend to care for what was required. Hunting was serious, like a book, but Wade didn't fret over the dangers of hunting because he knew how to handle a gun.

Wade had no map to Uncle Andrew's trailer, not even a map to the town, but he could find Vermont. Wade remembered the river that made the border with Vermont because a couple of years ago he and his father had driven for over an hour in the dark from Newfound to the wooded hills above that river. Rising light from behind them had shadowed his body long toward the river, which ran wider than Wade's familiar Winnipesaukee in Newfound. Even exaggerated, his dark self hadn't crossed a little of it, as if he were a bewitched spirit that haunted the horror novels he read.

By then he'd carried his own double barrel shotgun, bought with money from Uncle Andrew. They had seen no deer that day, fired no shots except to unload their guns at noon by shooting into a tree, as was his father's custom. "Always get one shot off," his father had said, "to make sure your gun's empty and to make sure they know you're there." On the way home his father, grumpy and tired, had kept saying that all the goddamn deer had gone to Vermont. Since they'd moved to Rumford, turning ugly had become his father's custom, as much as emptying his gun into a tree, only he didn't hunt anymore.

After class Wade brought his Withdrawal From School Form to the main office. Before Mr. Greenberg's secretary could ask any questions, he hurried out to the hallway. There stood Maria.

"My luck's holding today," he said. "Do you have a free period soon?" She told him third period. "My luck really is holding. I'm free then, too. Can you meet me in the caf? I'll buy you a Coke." Only after she agreed did he remember that his mother had taken all his money. As Maria walked away, he felt his luck evaporate. From his pocket he took the chocolate stained, napkin-map to Maria's place, soft and warm, worth more than the money his mother had taken, holding more luck than he'd just lost. Pressing it to his face, he smelled Maria, the soft darkness of her hair, the yellowy floral scent of her perfume.

"Don't do coke at school, Rule," Shawn Burns said.

Wade felt his face redden. He pocketed Maria's napkin and moved off to class.

Built like a fireplug, Shawn had never given up the junior high taunting, teasing everybody, even teachers. Short though he was, Shawn carried an energetic viciousness that made Wade uneasy. John said Shawn's older brother's beatings had toughened Shawn because no one can hurt you after your own family does you in. Shawn was not mature enough to understand about love. If Wade were to tell him about taking a trip with Maria, Shawn would wise off about drug trips.

Long ago Wade's mother had wanted to take a trip with no hunting, just to look at trees. The night before, his father, laughing hoarsely and throwing him roughly, dropped him. In between snuffles, Wade showed his mother the scraped flesh on his knee where he bashed the table corner.

"Don't make a fuss," his mother told him. "You'll spoil

our romantic trip tomorrow."

"Where are we going?" he asked.

"You'll see," she said.

They drove so far Wade lost track of where they were. When they stopped, his father picked him up under the armpits and tossed him into the air above his head where Wade could see the trees with white puffballs in their branches, tree after tree running down the hill. Falling back into his father's arms, he cried out fearing his father might drop him again. Again from high in the air he saw the magic lines of trees with sweet, sweet puffballs covering them like fancy ladies going to a ball in the picture book Uncle Andrew had given him. Again he cried out as he fell, though this time too his father caught him. Fear of crashing mixed with the delight at the trees' beauty.

"Put him down, Frank," his mother said. "You're making him scream."

Wade asked, "What are all those pretty trees? Daddy's lady trees?"

His mother's face, twisted with laughter, swooped down to his face. "That's for us to know and you to find out," she said. She laughed grindy hard, turning funny into mean. "The kid's got grand visions, Frank. Lady trees!"

Now, walking down the school corridor, Wade still had grand visions, though he had no money. When he got to the cafeteria, Maria said it was her turn to buy the Cokes. Then Wade knew his luck was holding. He touched the napkin in his pocket. For Maria, being a lady meant you shared with a man, even expenses and responsibility. Maybe that was what his mother had missed all these years.

Wade told Maria when he thought of ladies, he thought of Ms. Plizak, who was neither snobby nor phony. Wade said Ms. Plizak wouldn't turn her back on friends if some big thing happened to make her famous. She wouldn't change. That was the big mistake people made— they changed. Even after the accident had mangled Uncle Andrew, he hadn't changed inside. In the horror stories that Wade read, he could see people revealed for monsters. "Like my mother."

Maria said, "She's your mother, not a monster."

"She crippled my uncle," he said.

"How?"

"She made him have an accident on his motorcycle."

"Deliberately?"

"It ended up the same," he said. "Anyway, it was her fault."

Wade wanted to keep the conversation going. He had never told Ms. Plizak about his mother being a monster or even talked to her about horror stories. Ms. Plizak liked his hunting stories. He would try a different subject with Maria.

"You know what I saw on the chalkboard of my first period class?" he said. "SATAN or GOD. I wondered if it were a question or an answer."

Maria's eyes shifted when he looked at her. Should he tell her the truth about his feelings or just trust that she could sight them on her own?

"Do you go to church?" she asked.

"I have my own beliefs," he answered, "though maybe you'd call them foolish."

"I don't think you're foolish, Wade," Maria said. "I think you're lonely." Reaching across the table, she patted the top of his hand.

He would tell her a million stories if she'd touch him like this after each one, a touch as soft as tanned deerskin, like the buckskin gloves he'd given his father from the deer he shot.

"That's what you need now," she said, "family to support you."

"I need to look after Uncle Andrew." I'll be a lighter of the world, he thought. It seemed too bold a claim to make to Maria. He meant to take care of her too, both of them living at Uncle Andrew's trailer, where they could eat cinnamon toast and on Sundays go to church.

"You're such a good person, Wade." She drank from her Coke, then petted his hand again. "My father's family won't have anything to do with him, so I don't know them. They all live near Boston. The only one of my mother's family around here is my grandmother. She can't do much except encourage me to leave home. She blames my father for my mother's death."

Wade wondered why Maria didn't use the more exact word "suicide." Even after all these years, just the mention of it must still hurt. She drew her lips in as if she were holding back bitter spit, forcing herself to swallow it. With a couple of jerky movements, he reached for her hand and patted it. He wanted to hold it, press it to his cheek, but she gently pulled it away. Lips still lined together, she widened her mouth and eyes in an attempt to smile.

During his next class, Wade thought he did have family, but they couldn't help him. His mother had fixed that too. Long before Uncle Andrew's accident, Wade's family had driven off one Saturday night. As they traveled in the dark, Velma's snarling brown words about Frank Rule's hick family pushed away the sleep that kept trying to curl around Wade in the back seat. Almost immediately after arriving at a farmhouse, Wade was put upstairs in a cold, narrow bed in a cold, narrow room, a room full of creaks and squeaks like floorboards trying to pull apart. All night, voices crowding, laughing, shouting crawled up the walls and seeped into his room. A wondrous world sung underneath him.

At the breakfast table the next morning sat Uncle Andrew, Uncle Warren and his fat wife, Aunt Millie, and more of his father's family. His father had told him relations were complicated.

"Too complicated to explain to you," his mother said,

and with a pinch on his upper arm she shifted him to a chair near the end of the table.

For a while he watched a pile of doughnuts shrink, an iron skillet full of eggs reveal its black bottom, and a stack of gooey brown toast shorten. He was hungry, though at home he didn't usually eat much breakfast, just a bowl of cereal with the hope the milk hadn't soured. His mother said that she worked too hard to watch any food thrown into the sink, and she had yet to see a child with appetite enough in the morning to eat a big breakfast. She herself ate bacon, eggs, but never milk, which she hated. She would never even smell it to see if had gone bad.

"Try some cinnamon toast, Wade." Uncle Warren, a tall man, passed the plate to him.

From the end of the table Aunt Millie said, "We have plenty more."

"Eat up or else all through church service your stomach will growl worse than our sour choir," Uncle Andrew told him.

They smiled as he ate. He liked the eggs and especially the cinnamon toast, whose sweet-spicy, crunchy softness he hadn't tasted before. His aunt brought two more slices of the toast, fresh, thick, and warm. "If we kept Wade on this place a week," she told Wade's father, "we'd fatten him up proper."

These people, his relatives, his family, smiled often and deep, like Uncle Andrew. Wanting to please them, Wade sat up bright and alert beside his fat aunt in the long narrow plain building that was their church. In the sanctuary the boys all wore dress pants and shirts with dark ties tucked into their belts, the girls wore dresses and fancy shoes. Wade's worn jeans and faded tee-shirt made him conscious of his clothes for the first time in his life. Much as he liked this family, he felt as if he might be sent to the corner. Go stand in the corner until you stop crying, his mother used to tell him. After a while, he'd go without being ordered.

In the church they sang songs from a black book, Aunt Millie singing as loudly as the people in the choir. Their voices sounded hollow, as though they shouted through a pipe, which was why Uncle Andrew had called them sour. The words seeped into his head like the muffled talk that had come into his room last night, words he didn't know. The minister's sentences, long and swooping with twists and turns like an old path through thick woods, flowed on and on with no landmarks, no open view. Only one part slipped into a bright clearing. Wade heard the minister say, "I am the lighter of the world." Aunt Millie put her heavy arm around his shoulders and squeezed him. She smelled of sweet, warm, buttery cinnamon toast. When he looked at her smile, he realized he'd stared at the minister's mouth so long that his neck hurt. The lighter of the world meant smiles and hugs and kind words could light the world. Wade smiled at the minister.

Other children in the church didn't look at the minister.

A little girl in front of him played with her dress. At the end of his pew, a boy about his age closed his eyes. Maybe they already knew about lighting the world. Wade too felt sleepy. He clenched his fists so he could stay awake for Aunt Millie and her smile, no matter how difficult it was. On and on the minister's sermon traveled, wandering tangled woods without end. Then, suddenly, everyone stood, sang, and bowed their heads before leaving. Had Wade slept? No, no he hadn't.

He hoped he would get to stay a week with his relatives, but after church his parents said good-bye to Aunt Millie and Uncle Warren and Uncle Andrew. In the car on their way home Wade's mother told his father, "If your smarmy sister-in-law knows what's so wonderful for kids, she should have had a few of her own."

His father said, "She was just trying to make Wade feel at home."

"I don't have to travel that far for the pleasure of being sneered at and insulted," his mother said. "Fatten him up—just look at her, that cow. She still blames me for your divorce."

Wade never saw that family again.

Shane

Thursday night Wade dreamed of danger everywhere. Dressed in black, he strapped on pearl-handled revolvers and walked into the big room, where everybody shut up the minute he entered. Only the clatter of forks falling on plates broke the silence. A creepy feeling at the base of his skull ran up his scalp. He spun, pulled his revolver and squeezed the trigger, once, twice, killing them both. He knew they would have tortured him, mutilated him, and killed him, even if he never saw their faces.

Wade had read *Shane* in Mr. B's English class. Some of the kids had complained because they had to read a whole book. To them it didn't matter if the book ran a hundred pages like *Shane* or over four hundred, like a Stephen King book; a whole book was too long. *Shane* had taken Wade about three periods of sitting in the school library to read. Wade hadn't expected that the mother, a married woman, would have the hots for Shane, not in an old book. He had also been surprised that most of the kids in the class didn't even catch on that she had the hots for the gunslinger. Maybe it was too subtle for them because they'd watched too many dirty movies on their VCRs. Mr. B joked that they must not have gotten the illustrated version. Wade laughed aloud at that until he saw Dave, the kid next to him, thumbing through his copy looking for pictures.

This week Mr. B had shown the movie. He had said Alan Ladd, the actor who played Shane in the movie, was short, so Wade believed his dream had fit himself with no exaggeration, no phony Rambo lies. Although in the movie Alan Ladd wore blue, in his dream Wade had worn black and had sported pearl-handled revolvers, like Shane in the novel. Even in his dreams Wade stayed accurate.

At the end of the book Shane rode away from the valley with his life leaking out of him. Walking around with your gun carried a risk, just as trying to live your dreams did because dreams disguised danger, more danger than anyone could imagine. That was why Wade had to ride away, at least as far as Vermont.

Shane reminded Wade of the movie *The Road Warrior*, which he had seen at Peter's house. Peter was always renting movies and would copy them for you if you asked him on his two VCRs, though Wade never asked since he didn't have a VCR. Often Peter's parents spent weekends at their lake house and didn't care if Peter had friends over, unlike Wade's mother, who told him he could never have anyone in the house if she weren't home.

Peter lived in a nice house on the hill behind the high school with the rich people, the doctors and the lawyers, but he didn't dress like a snob nor did he act like one. In the basement of his house was a big room with a thin green carpet like they used on steps to imitate grass growing right up to your house. Peter had set up his own TV and VCR and stereo down there in front of a long couch. His bedroom, landscaped with comic books, was right off the big carpeted room. There was another room too with a furnace and a sink and a washer and dryer.

"My mother says I can be a custodian," Peter told Wade when he showed Wade around, "but I don't do laundry."

"We go to the laundromat," Wade said. "I mean my mother does. I don't go anymore. She tried to make me keep going, but I told her, kid stuff."

Actually, every week Wade lugged laundry the two blocks to the laundromat. He hated having to handle his mother's underwear in public, but if he brought any clothes back unfolded, she'd make him fold them while she watched, and that was even worse.

Saturday night Peter invited Wade to watch a dirty movie. "I'm eighteen," Peter told Wade, "so I won't get the video store in trouble for renting flesh flicks to me."

Peter never got anybody in trouble though he looked as if that were his main purpose in life. His black hair shagged over his collar, his whiskers poked rudely around zits, and his deep voice paused and rocked over words until he reached a laugh. Peter really liked to laugh.

While the flesh flick ran, Wade worried he'd get a hard-on. The movie's crime plot required no imagination. Watching it with another guy embarrassed Wade, but if Maria'd been there, he wouldn't've watched it at all.

After the movie ended, Peter said, "You know what's really dumb?"

Wade didn't like answering rhetorical questions. At school some kids were so eager to have their hands in the air and their names called that they answered everything the teacher said. A month ago in social studies class, Mac had said, "You remember yesterday when we talked about—" and this short, preppy girl had interrupted him before he even finished. "I remember yesterday." Mac had said, "Oh, great, another Beatles fan."

Wade had told this to Ms. Plizak, who'd said that girl would trip on her own feet while running over other people. Then Ms. Plizak had told him that Mac himself was a big Beatles fan and dealt in Beatles memorabilia. Wade thought it unusual for a teacher not only to be a fan but to buy and sell souvenirs.

"What's really dumb," Peter said, "is the way they roll credits, just like this were a real film." He used terms like *film* and *roll credits* since he'd taken the film course from Mr. B., but he didn't sound phony. He slid his hand over the scattered whiskers on his cheek. "I think the laws or unions require the credits to make it look like a real movie."

"It is real," Wade said. "People walking around, saying things, and getting paid for it. That's what life is." And the sex but Wade didn't want to talk about the sex. What he'd said about life had already made him too mad, or scared.

Peter said, "You want to smoke a joint?"

Wade said he would. He knew Peter was no burn-out, which, funny as it seemed to Wade, made him feel comfortable smoking with Peter. When had Wade last smoked a joint? Back in Newfound when he and Ernie had ripped off one from Ernie's brother's stash. Ernie, who smoked cigarettes, had shown Wade how to inhale. Five years later he still remembered how, so he knew he didn't look like a geek when he toked.

Peter giggled. A few tokes and he giggled. Now his hand reached way up into his hair, then he held it out in front of him. "Remember that movie *Road Warrior*?" This time he didn't wait for Wade to answer. "Remember when the nerdy motorcycle guy sticks up his hand to catch the metal boomerang and it knocks his fingers off? Look." Peter pulled his hand from his hair and holding it in front of his face slowly disappeared all the top joints. "I got it! I got it!" he shouted and giggled behind his fake mangled hand.

"That movie reminds me of *Shane*." Wade floated with his thoughts. Peter's giggles funneled softly as though they came through neon tubes. "A gunman, stranger, rides into a kind of war, saves the good guys, goes off at the end." Of course he knew more about the *Road Warrior* character than about Shane because he'd seen *Mad Max*, the movie that told how Max's family got killed. With Shane you didn't know anything about his life which made him mysterious. Wade liked that.

"Just like *Shane*, *Road Warrior* has a voice telling it, a narrator." Peter took up his idea. "And just like in the book, it's the kid."

"That'd be awesome." Wade talked rapidly but clearly now. "Wearing a gun like that big pistol Max has, nobody'd mess with you."

Peter's giggles faded, thinned, like clothes washed too many times, like Wade's clothes. Wade's mother had told him if he took care of them, they'd last longer.

"I'd stick that pistol in my mother's face, in her mouth, right in her maw," Wade said. His father must have done it like in the X-rated film they'd just watched otherwise he wouldn't be Wade's accidental father—down her throat with the barrel and squeeze the trigger. Bullets, large caliber hollow points, not just to penetrate, blow her maw all to hell. Her goddamn stinking, rotten maw.

"I don't like guns," Peter said. "Not in real life." He still giggled but with a squeak.

"They're okay if you know about 'em," Wade told him. "Like I do."

Dangling a strip of film, Peter said, "Look what I rescued."

It was a preview for a movie, thirty-five millimeter not videotape, a Disney movie. Wade inspected the individual frames, staring at the Magic Kingdom and the shots of a dog running in the woods. "Where d'you get it?"

For a moment Peter looked down, his hand rising as

if to retrieve the film from Wade, then rising higher, it reached his prickly chin. He smiled. "At the old drive-in."

"Where's that?"

"It's been closed for years. I'll take you there if you want to go."

Wade held the film to the light to scan through the woods scene. A bear appeared and reared back on his hind legs, threatening the dog. Since this was a Disney movie, Wade knew the dog wouldn't be hurt, but Wade knew what really happened to feisty little dogs who ran up against live bears in the woods.

"Maybe I can find some film for myself." Or for Maria, he thought. It'd make a great present.

Walking back home, Wade swore he'd never smoke grass again. It made him talk too much, talk about his mother's evil maw, which could land him deep in trouble. Beyond Cumby's parking lot loomed the high school like a dark mountain, gray stone that could rise up out of a camouflaged landscape, swallow you, and slop you around with gurgling digestive juices. The roots of plants and grass and trees that grew on the monster's surface, worms, and blind white grubs would all try to suck out your eyes so you'd turn as blind as they were. You wouldn't know what happened in the woods, you wouldn't see the world for what it was, you wouldn't believe that bears only shit in the woods.

"Training for the adult world comes early," Mac had

joked in American Culture. "You learn to live your life in advertising."

After class Wade went to Mac and said, "Maybe there ought to be a television show *The Wonderful World Of Adults* like the old Disney show. It could open with the adult Magic Kingdom and show nothing but ads."

"There is a show like that," Mac told him. "It's the shopping network."

The following week Mac assigned the class group projects to make commercials showing what they thought would be real in adult life. Wade couldn't come up with anything. He just sat off to the side of his group and listened while they debated about whether to emphasize sex or money. Wade couldn't imagine telling these kids the realities of an adult life like Uncle Andrew's, nor would they want to advertise those realities. He was afraid he'd catch hell for not participating. Mac told him, "Wade, you don't need to come up with anything. You came up with the whole idea in the first place."

Wade wished he could come up with an idea for a car right now. John didn't have the money for a car, and Peter, who had money, had failed the driving test twice and refused to take it again. Wade hadn't saved the money to pay for the driver's ed course. The only idea he could come up with was Riley. They didn't show that kind of solution on television or teach it in school either. They showed kids stealing cars, but Wade wasn't stupid. He knew how far you got in a stolen car.

Who
Are You?

Steam from the Hobart dishwasher clouded Wade's vision. Not that it mattered because he knew all these routines by touch and could wash dishes if he were blind. Leaving the house this morning without the retching smell of yeasty, sweet grease and smoke had put him in a good mood. Sunday morning, his mother slept in, his father slept it off. He hadn't seen them last night, hadn't seen them this morning. The steam cleared, and he sent another rack of dirty dishes into the machine.

The bad thing was Maria didn't work today. Why was it whenever he worked the same day as Maria, his mother worked that day too? He wondered if his mother scheduled it like that just to keep her hooks in. She always kept her hooks in trying to paralyze him.

After work Wade planned to walk to The Mills to see Maria. Although he'd try to hitchhike, he had no faith in getting a ride. He'd tried to hitch to Newfound to see Ernie once, walked ten miles, almost halfway there, then turned around and walked ten miles home. Thank God The Mills was only five miles. He'd walked that far hunting. He'd take Coke and chips to Maria and tell her about the abandoned drive-in Peter was going to show him.

In the dense steam, a hand touched his shoulder.

He jumped, skinning and burning his knuckles on the machine's hot metal. It was Rich, his boss, who said he wanted to see Wade during his break. Wade liked Rich, but he wanted to use his break time to call Maria and tell her he was bringing picnic-in-a-bag. Picnic-in-a-bag, a Sunday communion fit for God's clown. They both could use a laugh. That was for sure.

Rich, a heavy, dark haired man, was all business and sweat. "That's why his restaurant works," Wade's mother had told Wade. "That and he's loyal to his employees and doesn't listen to malicious gossip about them."

At ten-thirty Wade stepped into the small room that was Rich's office, a room with no desk, just a table, telephone, and several chairs. As usual Rich was standing, but he told Wade to sit.

"Wade, your mother tells me you might be quitting school."

On the wall were pictures of Rich and his staff, the cooks, the hostesses, the waiters, and waitresses, and the dishwashers, his "work family." A big photograph with Rich flanked by two waitresses, one of them Wade's mother, took up the center spot. Wade nodded his head, as much at the picture as at the still standing Rich.

"I have to tell you, you may think it's none of my business, but—" As Rich talked to Wade about his own quitting school and joining the Navy and how hard life bore on him because he hadn't graduated from high school and how much harder it was now for someone who quit school, Wade looked at the pictures, at all the people smiling, even in the Polaroid shot of himself standing in the steam by his machines; he had a silly grin like somebody'd just goosed him.

"If you quit school, you can't work here," Rich said. "The other thing is I need to see your grades. Report cards come out in a couple of weeks, your mother told me. I want to see all C's or better." Rich put his arm around Wade's shoulder. "I'm not being a hardass, but I don't want any young guy like yourself going through what I had to. You understand me? I'm not knocking the Navy. They taught me how to cook. But there were a lot of things I could have learned easier, and a lot of things I had to unlearn." A hand on each of Wade's shoulders, the big man waited for an answer.

"Yes, Rich."

"Good, get back to your job. You're a good worker, and your mother's a good woman; otherwise, I wouldn't take this time with you. I got a long list of guys willing to wash dishes."

Wade wished all those guys on Rich's list were here right now, taking turns at the machine while he went on his way to Maria's. Men like Rich, good guys at heart, always forgot that they'd been young. He'd heard a couple of Rich's stories about shore leave in Japan and figured Rich would never regret those times. Rich wanted to make

Wade forty years old to improve his attitude and turn his life around. That was Rich's part in it.

His mother, though, he couldn't understand because she hadn't acted logically, consistently. If he lost this job, he wouldn't earn any money to contribute to the household expenses she roared about like a dragon with its egg. If he graduated from high school, he would move out, first thing. Then she'd get nothing. Her behavior mystified him. Maybe it was love, her trying to save him from the scrounge jobs his father was limited to. Wade figured that if she were trying to do some good, it would come out absurd and illogical. He knew that love confused people. At Uncle Andrew's church the minister had talked about love that passed all understanding. That was good mystery. His mother made bad mystery, inexact, messy.

Tired, his hands smarting in the cold afternoon air, Wade walked the three blocks home. Passing Christos's Variety, the neighborhood store, he realized he couldn't go in and buy chips and Coke. He didn't even have money for lunch tomorrow. He'd demand money from his mother. She couldn't just take his pay as if he were a little kid.

Joe Christos himself waved a skinny hand at Wade. Wade was always struck by the covering of wrinkles, freckles, and thick white hairs on Joe Christos's hand. Wade waved back. Joe was okay. Sometimes when Wade bought peanut butter cups or crackers, he'd tell Wade to take an extra pack for being such a good, quiet boy in the store and never trying to swipe anything. John had told Wade that all the kids swiped things from the store because it was so easy. "Then what's the challenge?" Wade had asked. He never stole from Christos's. He even returned the extra money when Joe gave back the wrong change.

Neither his mother nor his father was home when he got to the apartment because they had gone to visit her mother in the nursing home. He wanted to blame his mother for forcing his father to drive on his day off, but he felt guilty for not visiting his grandmother. He was glad he worked Sundays. One Sunday his mother had left him off the work schedule so he could visit his grandmother. The emaciated body, the drooling, babbling, and cursing had horrified him. Devastatingly clearly, she called Velma, "You whore, you little bitch." Velma had stroked her mother's hand and cried. On the way back to Rumford she'd told Wade she saw that visiting his grandmother was too hard on him.

Lighting up Uncle Andrew's life he could understand. And Maria's. Not his grandmother's. She had left life. Why couldn't his mother see that? Trying to light the impenetrable dark confused his mother, led her into mysteries that raised her anger, even if she thought it was love. They said Christ could raise the dead, but Wade knew his mother couldn't.

Now Wade couldn't demand money from his mother, now he had nothing to buy Coke and chips with, now he was stuck. If he arrived at Maria's empty-handed, what would he say? I was in the neighborhood and thought I'd drop in? How could he convince her to go to Vermont with him if he couldn't even come up with the price of a Coke?

His hair, steamed from the dishwasher, felt clammy. A long, roaring yell blasted from his lungs and filled the apartment. Rushing into his room, he ripped *The Shining* poster from his wall. The glossy, crinkling paper ball bounced off the floor and rolled under his bed as if it were hiding from his wrath. With a tight grip on his own arms, he sat on the bed, shrieked one last time, and lay back to stare at the ceiling.

From behind the wall came scratching from the fleet mouse his mother claimed ruined her nights. It ran part way up to where the movie poster had been. Wade slid from the bed, loaded his shotgun with birdshot, and took quick aim. The rustling started again, and before the mouse could gain a foot, Wade squeezed the trigger. Pellets ripped through the plaster board, filling the room with white chalky dust. Pieces of wall stuck in his hair and freckled his face, making him itch. He put the shotgun down. Pressing his ear to the wall, he couldn't hear any scurrying mouse. He must have killed it. In a week they'd know for sure by the smell, but by then he'd be gone.

Smoothing out *The Shining* poster as best he could, he tacked it up to hide the mess he'd blown in the wall. In the bathroom he stuck his head under the shower hose to blast away the plaster debris. When she found it, his mother would probably send him a bill at Uncle Andrew's. She shouldn't charge him. He'd killed the miserable mouse for her, hadn't he? He laughed. God, it felt good to laugh, even at himself.

Money. In her purse. He dried his face and hair and hurried to his parents' bedroom. On her bureau sat a hard blue purse, empty except for a nearly finished pack of Salems and some crumpled pink tissues. Of course she'd taken money for a restaurant meal. She'd say, "Just because I waitress doesn't mean I don't like to eat out as much as the next woman. Surprise me one time, Frank, take me out without my asking."

Maybe in the kitchen Wade could find Coke to take to Maria's. The refrigerator revealed a rack of beer, a bottle of his mother's pink wine that she almost never drank, and a quart of milk, probably turning sour. Pushing shut the door, he saw a black purse perched on the counter. Expecting more half-empty cigarette packs and pink tissues, he spread it open and peered inside, keeping his fingers out of it. Her wallet, red and hard, lay on top of the usual junk. He drew it out, opened it, and took a ten dollar bill, which would feed him until payday. Maybe not. After buying Coke and chips for Maria, he'd still have four lunches to buy. He took another ten and jammed them both into his jacket pocket. He'd find a better hiding place for them later. He wasn't going to be stupid enough to stick them in his wallet so she could snatch them from him again.

Passing Christos's, Wade saw Joe's wrinkled hand wave again. He'd planned to buy the chips and Coke in the strip mall at The Mills so he wouldn't have to carry a bag all the way. Maybe people'd be afraid to give him a ride if he carried a bag. It was clear thinking, but he felt disloyal to wave to Joe and head off to spend his money at another store.

"Big party?" Joe asked as he bagged Wade's stuff.

"A picnic," Wade told him, "with my girlfriend."

"She's a lucky girl."

By the time he got to Main Street, the bag weighed heavy on his arms. He couldn't grip it by the top because the thin paper would tear. He could have grabbed a plastic supermarket bag at home, but he hadn't planned. Sticking out his thumb, he walked toward The Mills, not looking at the drivers that passed him but hoping they'd see his walking as a sign of ambition.

He shifted the bag from arm to arm. At least his conscience wasn't heavy. No way. That was his money he'd taken. He hadn't planned to take it, but he hadn't planned that his mother would take it from him either. Why hadn't he expected it? It didn't matter anymore anyway. She did what she needed to, and he'd do the same. She'd taught him her way. "You've got two hands," she'd say. "Use them."

Across from the prison, a mile from town, signs posted a warning: PRISON ZONE—DO NOT PICK UP HITCHHIKERS. He didn't even look at the cars as he walked, afraid he'd see every one as a perfect ride. Four more miles stretched before him as the bag grew heavier. He tried thinking of it as a gun, carried as he walked through the woods, his mind so focused on the deer he would shoot that the gun seemed only an extension of his arm with no more weight than his hand. Walking quietly, quickly through the morning woods, stepping through fresh red leaves and sometimes on a white dust of snow, hoping for prints or pellets, brought him joy. Hunting made him as happy as when he had visited Uncle Warren and Aunt Millie.

In November he'd take Uncle Andrew hunting. He would find a place where he could push the wheelchair to set Uncle Andrew in a stand while he drove deer past him. In Vermont they'd use rifles because they'd be out of the city limits, at least he thought they would. Uncle Andrew's trailer was out of the city. His father always said there weren't any cities in Vermont because Vermont had more cows than people.

Wade had walked another two miles and hadn't run out of the sight of houses. No matter where you walked in Rumford, you were always within sight of houses. There was always someone to watch you. Uncle Andrew said people watched you instead of watching over you.

Wade hoped Uncle Andrew owned one of those folding wheelchairs they could stow in a car trunk when they went hunting; otherwise, they'd have to buy one of those handicap vans with the ramp and wide doors. Unless you could rent one. Wade had noticed handicapped vans from the county and social agencies transporting people around Rumford. Maybe Vermont had the same service. Once he got there, he would check out all these details. Of course he'd have to get a driver's license.

An hour of mostly level walking had brought him four miles out, right by the fire station. Passing the wide driveway, he didn't hitch, but when he reached the other side, he thumbed the first car that came, an old blue station wagon that stopped for him. In it were Dave, the short-haired, wide-eyed football player from his English class, and Dave's father, a man who'd rather fish than sleep, or so Dave had told Wade many times.

"I asked my father to stop for you. I didn't know you lived out here."

"Girlfriend," Wade said. The car smelled of dog, wet and moldy. A matting of hairs covered the seat next to Wade. He thought of Scout, his German shepherd that his mother had killed.

"Wade says there's not enough wild country in Rumford," Dave told his father.

"He should try Rattlesnake Hill." Dave's father, a big man who gripped the wheel with strong, red hands, laughed. "Course there aren't any rattlers up there if that's what he's after."

"It's where the quarries are," Dave said.

Wade had heard of them, places where kids drank and swam. He'd ask John about it, thinking it could be a place to go if Vermont didn't work out.

At Maria's with bag in arm, grown heavy again, Wade rang the bell for Blanchard, one long ring, then waited. After a while he rang again, two short rings. The door between the foyer and the hallway blocked the view with frosted glass etched with flowers. The long stems and flowing petals running up the sides reminded him of church windows. He tried the knob, and though it didn't turn, the door opened.

Dark greeted him, and the smell of cooked cabbage, a heavy smell that pressed warm and smothery in his nose. Along the walls ran wainscoting of nearly black wood. He held the bag tighter, as if he might drop it, the Coke exploding, the chips spreading all over the floor. Counting gold numbers on doors led him to the second floor, where he found #14.

Television noise along with a woman's voice speaking baby talk came from behind the door. Wade knocked. His hand hit the thin panel harder than he'd intended, rattling it as if he might break the door. A fat woman of about forty wearing a checkered skirt and a tank top opened the door. Saying nothing she looked down the apartment hall, which was filled with cardboard boxes piled nearly to the ceiling. Dark, gray-streaked hair lay sweat-plastered to her face.

"You want him?" she asked.

"Maria."

From down the hall strode a bare-chested man in dark blue dress pants, a baby in his arms. His arm muscles swelled as he handed the child to the woman.

"Maria ain't here," he said. He wiped his forehead as if to smooth hair that wasn't there. Wade figured him to be Maria's father. "You got some books or something for her?" He reached for the bag.

"No, I—" Wade pulled the bag away. He felt his face flush. He was being a moron. "Do you know when she'll be back?"

The man leaned against the door. Clearly a head taller than Wade, he looked down, his mouth twitching between a grin and a cry. "I don't know where she goes." His body blocked the doorway, the man could be hiding Maria to keep Wade from seeing her. "Who are you?"

"Wade. Wade Rule."

The man straightened, looked down his crowded hall, then back at Wade. "I never heard of you."

The Drive-In

On Monday Mr. B passed out this assignment to Wade's English class:

SHANE – ESSAY TOPIC – ENGLISH 11

Bob looks to both his father and Shane as role models, people to teach him how to be an adult. Are there any such people in your life? Why did you choose them? Which of their qualities do you hope to emulate? Write about 300 words. Be specific. Focus on not more than two people.

Connie, a short, lively girl who liked to get paper for everybody, put a blank sheet in front of Wade. Dave told Mr. B he wanted to write about his father, the man who had given Wade the ride yesterday. Wade was glad Dave didn't ask him anything about Maria.

"My father because—" Dave said.

"Don't tell me," Mr. B said. "Get it down on paper, and then I'll look at it."

Why did teachers always say "look at it" instead of "read it"? At least Mr. B really read what students wrote and didn't just look to see if they kept busy darkening white paper with black or blue ink. Last year's math teacher made Wade worksheet crazy, always more problems, filling up the page with erasable ink numbers, as if they mattered to anyone. She was not a role model.

Mr. B said they should have someone in the class read their paper, which he called "peer editing." Connie, bouncy little Connie, nice and smart though she was, held her confidence like a shiny mirror. Dave puzzled Wade because he always asked for help though he always knew what he should do. Wade wished John were in his class because he'd show John what he wrote, though right now there was nothing to show—just white paper with thin blue lines running across it.

Wade took out his copy of *Nightshift*, opened it to his place, marked by a folded Reese's Peanut Butter Cup wrapper, and started to read. Mr. B tapped him on the shoulder. "Are you all done with your assignment?" No sarcasm lurked in the question, which Wade knew was not a question. The orange wrapper, folded flat as truth, slid back between the pages as Wade closed his book.

"Will I have to show it to other kids?" Wade asked.

Mr. B's hand left Wade's shoulder. He turned and looked down, full in Wade's face. "Did you read *Shane*?" he countered.

"I got a hundred on the test."

Mr. B backed up a step. "That's right," he said. He smiled, to make up for the accusation.

"I can't write this paper anyway," Wade told him. He flicked the stiff edge of the book mark with his finger. "I don't have any role models."

Mr. B sidled to the next desk. Words, warm, approving, indistinct, sounded. Did Mr. B know that Wade was lying, or was he trying to prove to Wade that whatever Wade wrote he would praise and keep confidential? Dave raised his hand for help, or maybe just to show off what he'd done. Below his short hair, Dave's eyes beamed, like the large liquid eyes of a deer. No. Not a deer. Nothing frightened or furtive. More like Wade's dog's eyes, the big German shepherd eyes, eyes that never held fear.

Even after his mother had said Scout was too sick to live, Scout's eyes showed friendship, warm brown friendship. "No more dogs," his mother had said. "I won't have all this fussing over a dead dog, and that's that." But Dave's eyes were blue, obviously blue, too obvious. Wade was glad he hadn't been born with such obvious eyes. How could anyone live with such obvious eyes? Wade couldn't help Dave any more than he could have saved Scout.

"Wade, why don't you write something?" Connie, with her ever twitching smile, stopped beside him. "I brought this paper for you to write on because I know you're so damn smart. I didn't waste my effort, did I?" She cocked her head and blinked flirtatiously. "Did I?"

"I won't show it to you," Wade said.

"Don't show me yours, I won't show you mine." Connie shook her butt and laughed her high pitched laugh.

"Connie's getting attention again," Jim said from the back.

Wade turned around. Jim wasn't writing anything. He was smart, but he never turned in any papers. Wade had watched Mr. B come around to collect papers and stand in exasperation in front of Jim. Even Jim and Connie managed to make themselves likable enough so they could break some rules without being thrown out of the game.

Wade felt like a deer. His father had told him that deer spent every minute guarding their lives. "You come out one November morning to shoot a deer, but they're all day, every day of the year, wary, watching, sniffing the breeze, feeling the ground under their feet for danger, enemies, death. That's why hunting's such hard work."

At school Wade kept watch, but it wore on him. He stayed wary like the deer. He knew if he told the complete truth, he'd be hurt. If he could let it out a little at a time, making jokes. He made sure no one was watching him before he wrote his first sentence.

If you have a gun, you don't need a role model.

He added another sentence.

What you need is power.

Power comes out of the barrel of a gun, where'd he heard that? In Mac's class, maybe. The point of *Shane*, the point of *The Road Warrior*, was to fight because there were always gunfighters out there or motorcycle gangs. Books and movies didn't say mothers. Maybe they didn't dare to. Or they didn't know.

So many of these kids were different from Wade

because they walked around as if they had the world by the ass. Even Peter, even John, they could always take two steps without worrying that the third one would trip them up. If he'd stayed in Newfound, kept hunting and fishing, his father would have been his role model. He wrote more sentences.

People change. You can't depend on them. You trust them and like them and they change. That's why I don't have a role model. That's why I don't want a role model. People are so complicated that you can never just sight one in and depend on it to fire true.

His father had said he didn't want to move from Newfound. His mother said if she had to commute to Big Rich's in Rumford, Wade would be by himself every afternoon. Besides, they could save gas money and maintenance on the car. And she knew Frank didn't enjoy driving an extra forty or fifty miles a day. "You've lived here all your life," she told his father. "The change will do you good."

Her narrow body blocked the archway to the living room. On the floor Wade leaned his head against the vinyl hassock with the blue and white pie-shapes while his father ran his hands up and down the stiff upholstery of the stuffed chair, as if he were trying to gain a handhold to yank himself upright. Wade felt it getting darker in the room and wondered why his mother didn't reach over to switch on the floor lamp. Standing in the dark his father liked, she wove the logic of her talk until she trapped his father into moving to Rumford. Maybe she hadn't known how much his father would change.

People change and I will too. No matter what you start out with, you give it up. People shouldn't make kids do what they don't want to do because they'll have a whole life of that. Kids think when they grow up they'll get to do what they want, but life's not like that. It's just the opposite. There's no sense in having a role model. You have to do it all yourself. You need your own dreams, not someone else's, then at least if you screw up, it's your screw up. If your dream hurts you, it's your dream doing the hurting.

Now what was he doing? Crying on paper, like a rabbit crying when the fox cornered it, giving away its position, revealing its weakness. Stupid. Rabbits were dumb. What did they think, other rabbits were going to come to save them? Wade looked at his paper. It didn't show fear. Not really. Why should it? Mr. B was a good guy, a good teacher. Dave had given him a ride. Connie gave him paper. It wasn't a place to be scared. It was just a place he didn't want to be. It was a place he couldn't do any good in. Hadn't he said that in his essay, more or less?

That afternoon Peter showed him the way to the old Rumford Drive-In. Along the mile to the lower bridge, Peter described the cut-off between the tire shop and the lumber yard, but when they crossed the river, Wade thought of the Newfound Flats, where the really poor kids lived jumbled up in old mill housing. He didn't pay attention to the auto dealership and restaurant, the busy businesses, because his mind was flooded with the memory of the Newfound river rats pushed along the banks of the Winnipesaukee.

"If we don't get out of this town," his mother had told his father, "we'll sink farther and farther, like mud sliding down a hill, until we end up in one of those River Street dumps." In this memory Wade discovered for the first time that his mother held her own fear.

Going past the commercial area made him edgy, as if he were trespassing and would fall into some trap. Still, Peter, no danger daring guy, had explored the place before, had even brought back filmstrips to prove it. Peter pointed to the sign at the entrance. An island of evergreen bushes grown wild covered the sign's lower supports. Under NOW PLAYING were the words FOR SALE OR LEASE and a Manchester phone number. High above the sign a pole bore a hooded light like some giant cobra that must have once shone bright on cars. Along the dirt road entrance stood tall trees, mostly willows and some other hardwoods, as well as bushes covered with the scraggly dead remains of old tent caterpillar nests. Stands of sumacs and swamp maples showed leaves gone rusty. A chain link fence jutted out of the weeds but stopped short of the road, its gate gone, its purpose long breached. Across from it lay a pole that had once formed a barrier. Farther along, a cable stretched over the ground, and the first of several battered, overturned shopping carts appeared, abandoned vehicles of the street people Peter said used to come here.

A dead gray late afternoon sun hung over the parking lot's churned ground, like some old battlefield. Rows of speaker poles painted red and blue lined the broken asphalt, some infantry company blown away at neck level. When he joked about this with Peter, Peter said he was thinking of parking meters, not speakers, which would have dangled on the side of the poles and didn't look like heads at all.

"Yeah, I know," he told Peter. "I swiped one once." Back in Newfound Ernie had shown him a drive-in speaker his brother had ripped off a pole and hooked up to his stereo. It had sounded tinny.

The concession stand, some thirty by forty feet with bathrooms at each side, raised its yellow cinderblock self up in the middle of the lot. Its door hung off one hinge, leaning into the ground like a dead man waiting to fall in slow motion. It was locked half open. That would make anyone inside vulnerable to attack, thought Wade, or safe, because the attackers might think the place empty. Considering the place for a camp made him examine it carefully, in ways Peter wouldn't think of.

On the floor, where some vinyl tiles still adhered, lay a dead rat. Wade knew it had lain there a long time because it didn't have the powerful dry sour smell of rotted meat. The place held very little smell, just the edgy odor of cold concrete, cinder block, and metal. The display case for candy held only jagged glass, not even wrappers.

"Nobody must come here," Wade said.

"I've never seen anyone," Peter said. "This is where I found the film."

He led Wade into the projection booth. No equipment remained in the room, but around the floor were scattered torn clips of film and one half of a reel case. Picking up a strip with three or four frames, Wade raised it to the cold light that slanted through the projection slit. The shot framed a man and a woman, two heads, there was probably a technical name for it that Peter knew, a name that would label it, but it would not label it for Wade, who thought of his mother and father, and then how wonderfully different he and Maria were. They were young. Maria was pretty. Neither of them lived on snarling anger the way his parents did. "Just you wait," his mother said, "and you'll find out what it's like when you're on your own." But Uncle Andrew was on his own, and he hadn't turned mean.

"Where's the screen?" Wade asked.

"Burned down. It's been gone a long time."

"Maybe somebody'll burn this."

"Nothing much to burn."

Anything would burn if you got it hot enough. From outside came the sound of laughter and metal whanging against the poles. Was it Herman, the street bum with his length of lead pipe and his machete hidden among the bedroll, clothes, and money in his shopping cart?

Peter put finger to lips, flapped his hand for them to

hunker down on the projection booth's cold concrete, and shrugged his narrow shoulders. If not Herman, one of the other street people, that crazy woman who swore at everybody with a lit cigarette dancing in her mouth? (Wade's mother seldom swore.) Or one of the owners? Though there weren't any NO TRESPASSING signs, if the owners inspected their property regularly, it would spoil the place for a hideout. The cart rammed against the cinder block wall. It must be Herman the bum.

The cockeyed door scraped as the outsider crowded inside, his laughter sounding like sharpening knives. "Any bums here?" the voice shouted.

Smells mingled, flame, quiet as from a butane lighter, sweet herbal smoke, and the bready, sour-yeast odor that came from Wade's father when he sat on the sad sofa and downed bottles of beer.

Wade, balanced on the balls of his feet, felt his calves cramp, his chest tighten from holding his breath. He took out the Case jackknife that he honed every day. He was exact in his duty, keeping himself and his knife prepared. Running his thumb the length of the blade's three inches tingled with the barely broken skin feel of beating blood. His heart shuddered.

"Herman's passed out from drinking Mad Dog," the sharp voice said. "He'll burn like a dead Christmas tree."

With neither door nor darkness to hide him, Wade charged out of the projection room and into Shawn Burns.

"Here's the bum!" Shawn's voice tin snipped as he tripped Wade.

Why hadn't Wade recognized Shawn's voice before, the voice that snapped insults sharp as a rat's tooth from his moon face? Keeping his knife hidden, Wade raised up to one knee.

"Don't pray to me." Shawn laughed his half-cocked giggle. "I'm not your god. I'm your Satan." Shawn took a longneck Rolling Rock from his backpack.

"Leave us alone," Wade told him as he stood.

Peter, quiet as dust, kept behind Wade.

"Don't start with me!" Shawn roared. Then he howled out a laugh. "Be a friend, Rule, drink a beer with me."

Wade had hated the sour taste of the beer his father'd made him drink years ago in Newfound.

"You try it," he told Wade, "then I won't have to worry about your swiping it behind my back." First a sip, then a swallow, until the whole glass jerked Wade's head dizzy, like a deer running crazed through a thicket of hunters.

"Is this the right way to treat friends?" Wade asked. The question shocked him as much as it did Shawn.

Shawn stared at Wade as though wondering how nuts or dangerous Wade might be. Tilting his head back, Shawn chugged from his beer. "You a holy boy?"

Wade knew you didn't turn your back on Shawn, who played tricks like cutting girls' hair when they passed out at parties or supergluing lockers. "We're all holy boys," Wade said, "only some of us are holy jerks."

"Don't worry about backwash. I'll get you a fresh beer." From his backpack Shawn pulled another longneck. "Don't you want to be friends with me?"

Wade wouldn't be told what to do, wouldn't have beer forced on him, wouldn't allow Shawn in a hideout where he would bring Maria. He held his knife underhand, fingers curled below the blade, ready to rip up through Shawn's belly. "Don't be a jerk, Shawn."

"Oh, be a fucking holy boy like you."

Wade flashed his knife. Bringing it before him, he held it tight, keeping the open blade a protective point. "Get out."

Shawn returned the unopened beer to his backpack. Wade wondered if he should fold his knife and take Shawn's hand. He knew he was in charge here.

Shawn said, "Don't—"

"Leave," Wade ordered.

After Shawn had gone, Peter said, "I know him. He won't be back."

On the way home hunger attacked Wade. At the same time nausea rose to the bottom of his throat and threatened him with the dry heaves his father sometimes fell victim to. How could he want to eat and puke at the same time? His mother always said she couldn't afford to get sick.

Stopping on the other side of the river, he looked back

over the valley, where pine trees hid the drive-in, even from a searching eye. Maybe it could work as a hideout until he could reach Uncle Andrew. He told Peter he was going to the restaurant to see Maria. He decided to call it a celebration.

Using some of the money he had taken from his mother's purse, he ordered tomato soup and neatly broke lots of crackers in his bowl. He never crumbled them because then they'd turn soft and soggy too fast, tasting as if someone else had already eaten them.

"Can't stay away from the place, huh?" It was Rich, finger polishing his moustache and patting Wade's shoulder.

There would be no dinner at home. "I didn't want to bother my mother."

"She told me you fix all your own meals."

"Just feeling lazy today." Wade held off floating more crackers. "Where's Maria?"

"She left early for an appointment. Bon appetite."

Glad not to hear another lecture about school, even a friendly lecture from Rich, Wade finished his soup and crackers. No longer hungry or nauseated, he walked home almost happy.

A frown ran his mother's eyebrows into a humped bunch. "Taking up stealing, have we?" The light tan top of her uniform wore so many creases and stains, she wouldn't get another day's wear out of it, maybe the darker brown skirt but definitely not the blouse.

"Have I got to do the laundry tonight?" Wade asked.

"Laundry," his mother said. "Let me see that wallet." Her hand, half-pointer half-fist, threatened what her mouth held secret. Her cheeks sucked in when she discovered his wallet empty, empty because Wade had hidden the money under the porch before he entered the house. "Are you buying drugs? I'll get you tested. You won't pee without a test if I catch you robbing me to buy dope."

"I don't do drugs." He reached for his wallet, but she shook it at him.

"You do steal though, don't you? The one day I leave my purse here, you're into it."

Wade mumbled a denial and reached for his wallet. Still she held onto it, like a dog gripping with its jaws. "Give me back my wallet."

"I'm not going to argue with Mr. Liar about taking my money, not when we have rent coming due." She released his wallet.

"Take it out of my next paycheck," he said.

"I could sell your shotgun and have the interest and penalty on that loan."

"You don't touch my gun!"

"You don't touch my purse!" Her voice jammed strong against his face. "Or anything that's not yours."

"Did I get any mail? Did I get a letter from Uncle Andrew?"

"If you'd come home this afternoon, you'd know the

answer to that. Only instead of being here to get the mail, pick up the house, and do your homework, you chose to go off and buy drugs with my money. You'll end up just like that druggy bum of an uncle of yours. Criticizing me when he can't even pay his own bills." She lit a cigarette and blew smoke from the corner of her mouth.

"You lie," he said.

"Call him up and ask him. Be my guest." Her thin lips pressed into a smile while more smoke escaped in narrow streams. "I'll even pay for the call."

Grease Trap

The next day in English class Dave, his obvious eyes shining, told Mr. B, "My dad read my paper last night. We both cried."

While Mr. B patted Dave's shoulder, Wade pulled his *Shane* essay from his backpack and crumpled it. As Mr. B explained that they would have a unit test tomorrow along with an in-class writing assignment, Wade wrote on a new sheet. *My Uncle Andrew is my role model even though he is in a wheelchair.*

Wade wrote about Uncle Andrew's giving him the motorcycle ride and taking him to Ernie's house. In Wade's words Uncle Andrew became an adventurous and daring man, always young, yet filled with wisdom, which he shared out of his fondness for Wade. Wade compared him to Shane's love for the boy, Bob, but wrote that Uncle Andrew was funnier than Shane. For a minute he tried to think of an example, then wrote that he was fun loving. *You'd have to get to know him to really understand why he's such a spirited person. He's in a wheelchair in Vermont, and I'm going to take care of him.*

When he handed it in, Wade felt satisfied with his paper even though he'd written it quickly. It wasn't bitter like the one he'd written first. He couldn't really be proud of that one. His new one would probably earn him a good grade. It would be great to tell Uncle Andrew he'd earned an A for writing about him as a role model.

As Mr. B reviewed for the test on a unit called *The Need To Be Free*, Wade wondered if Uncle Andrew had sent him a letter. Or called. He hoped Uncle Andrew wasn't sick. Even in his wheelchair, Uncle Andrew didn't look sick but strong, as if sitting there were only a joke and at any minute he would jump up, stick Wade in the ribs, and yell, "Rumpty-de-Dump!"

His mother said Andy would die from the drugs he took before any disease killed him, but since he never worked, he'd outlive them all. Wade's father said they weren't drugs, they were medication, and his mother said, "It's the same thing, and what's worse, since Andy's on Medicaid, I'm the one paying for them."

Envy always ate at her like a worm in her heart, like his dog's heartworm. "Scout's got heartworm," his mother'd said. "He's going to weaken and die."

"What about pills?" Wade asked.

"We can't afford pills for a dog."

Because she didn't have the courage to take a gun and shoot Scout, she paid the veterinarian to stick a needle in him. When Wade asked her how much that had cost, she didn't even answer him.

Wade knew he had the courage to kill when the time came. He'd shot his deer, hadn't he? No man's luck holds.

That's true, but his courage can hold, if he holds onto his courage. He'd faced down Shawn Burns, hadn't he?

When the bell rang, Wade knew he had to leave school for the day. He had work this afternoon, and he'd see Maria at work. Right now he was going home, taking time off for "personal business." He'd written that he would look after Uncle Andrew, so the time had come to start. Otherwise he'd be just another liar and a hypocrite.

At home he sat in front of the telephone staring at Uncle Andrew's number so long he memorized it. 802-555-2156. He repeated it without pressing a single button on the narrow telephone, a white and blue model his father had brought home from some promotion at work. "Even when you steal," his mother said, "you take something shoddy." If Wade was to take care of Uncle Andrew, he had to act, he had to call now. As deliberately as if he were squeezing a trigger, he pressed the buttons. Instantly, he heard the buzz of a ring, followed by a voice.

"We're sorry. To call this number, you must first dial a one. Please hang up and try again."

In his thinking, with all his memorizing, he'd screwed up. No waiting now, he pushed the numbers, starting with a finger flourish for the 1. Ring followed ring. Naturally, he'd wait for Uncle Andrew to wheel to the telephone. When he started working in Vermont, the first thing he'd buy would be a cordless telephone Uncle Andrew could holster right on his chair.

"The number you have reached, 802-555-2156, is not in service. No further information is available at this time."

It took him a minute to find the page in the phone book that explained how to call out-of-state information. In less than a minute he heard, "I show no listing under Andrew Rule, R-U-L-E. Is there another spelling? R-U-E-L?" Wade hung up. Either Uncle Andrew had moved or he had lost his phone for non-payment. "Welfare won't pay for a telephone," his mother had said, "that's why he hasn't called you." That's why she offered to pay for a call to Uncle Andrew last night.

Of course she knew about Uncle Andrew's phone because she'd taken Wade's letter. The one day he didn't come home to get the mail, the letter arrived for her to snatch. If she hadn't thrown it out or taken it with her, it must be in her bedroom. Even as he walked into the bedroom, he could feel his heart cringe, shame beating it with a nightstick. Why did he have to sin so much in order to do good? It must be one of God's tricks. Slim Jim's long arm would grab him, pinch his neck, take him to the station for torture.

The phone rang; the noise scared him, as if he'd set off a burglar alarm. Again it rang. He ran to it, lifting it more to shut it off than to answer it. But now holding it, he felt the heavy thud of guilt punch his chest.

"Hello?"

"Wade? Is this Wade Rule?" A woman's English accent

spoke accusation more than question. He mumbled his identity. "Why did you leave school today?"

"I was sick. I'm sick."

"You didn't go to the nurse, you didn't sign out, you didn't get a dismissal."

"I felt sick."

"Is one of your parents home?"

"Both are at work."

"You'll have to see Mr. Greenberg tomorrow."

"I'm sick."

"If you don't come to school tomorrow, you must have your parents call us before the beginning of classes."

He found himself holding his breath as he entered his mother's bedroom, as if his mother would dash out of the closet or spring from under the bed. "This is stupid," he said. Back to the telephone, he dialed the restaurant and asked for her. The cashier said she was busy, could she call back, and Wade hung up.

In the top drawer of her bureau, he found a package of Trojans. He pushed them aside with cloth, then realized he was holding her panties. Their shiny yellow slippery feel raised his neck hairs and turned his stomach sloppy.

Under her pillow lay her nightgown, like she was a little kid. She used to make him keep his p.j.'s under his pillow, but since he did the laundry and made his bed, she'd stopped paying attention to that. On her side of the bed was a nightstand, painted with gray porch enamel. It held

Vaseline and Vicks and some liquid for corns and a tube of Ben-Gay, all lined up so neatly; he bet she could pick out whichever one she wanted in the dark. His father had no nightstand, probably because she didn't trust him not to make mistakes. He'd made one big one already. He'd made Wade.

Opening the nightstand's drawer, he found the letter, a cream-colored envelope right on top, addressed to Wade Rule, 95 South State Street, Rumford, NH. The handwriting circled and arced in fancy curlicues, as if Uncle Andrew was showing off his artistic ability. Wade wondered if Uncle Andrew didn't know Rumford's zip code, then he saw he'd also left the zip code off his return address. Wade knew he'd done it on purpose because Uncle Andrew always acted exactly, even when he was having wild fun. Maybe it was a joke. Uncle Andrew said a sense of humor was a gift from God.

Dear Wade,

Good to hear from you, my favorite Rumpty-de-Dump nephew. Sorry to hear about your troubles. Things have been rough here too lately, especially since my lady love abandoned me. Where two paychecks covered the bills, one will not stretch so far, not by half. Maybe by twenty dollars less than half, to be strictly accurate. After all, I have little left but accuracy, especially when it comes to bills.

And to be strictly accurate, I can only offer you a visit, not a home, and a short visit at that. Wade, pained as I am to say so, I must be honest here. I just don't have the money. Two incomes, two people—yes. One income, one person—barely. One income, two people—no. Definitely no. You don't need the figures to do the math.

Now, don't let this cast your poor heart further into Sadville, Rumpty-de-Dump. Your wild gimpy uncle loves you as much as ever. He also remembers the teenage blues as well as anyone whoever memorized a phone number, which due to finances, I no longer have. What you need is to talk to someone, and I'll guess it isn't your mother. Your father's never been much of a talker. (Less a singer, only don't tell him I said so.) There must be a teacher or counselor at your school who'd give you a sympathetic ear and a wise tongue. Or maybe you know a minister in town, if your mother's changed her mind about church.

Find somebody, Wade. That's what kept me going through rehab, people to listen and listen to and God's love. Even now that my lady's love's gone, I keep my heart beating with love.

God bless you,
Uncle Andrew

He wants me to come there, thought Wade. He needs me to talk with and to help him out. That's what the letter's all about. Poor Uncle Andrew, just like him to keep his pride when he asked for help. Wade could do that math without the figures. There'd be two people and two incomes. Three people counting Maria, but that'd be okay. A little overtime would earn enough money to pay for her food. Oh yes, he had the right idea now. He was sure he had.

His stomach convulsed. Ripples of breath jumped in

his chest. His nose ran. From closed eyes his tears leaked. Finally came the sobs, choked back. He flopped onto the bed, hands clutching the soft frilly fabric. He cried and cried. The gasping slowed, stopped. He had control of himself. He raised himself from his mother's pillow and opened his eyes. He found himself clutching her nightgown. He shrieked as if he'd been bitten.

Hands shaking, he slid the letter back into the envelope, tucked it inside the nightstand, and pushed the drawer closed. The wood whispered like a frightened breath.

When he woke on his own bed, he had barely enough time to put on the work whites from the laundry service and walk to the restaurant. He wanted to talk to Maria. Uncle Andrew had written he should talk with someone who made him feel good.

As he popped his card into the time clock, he saw there were few dishes left to be washed. There was, however, much more to be done. Rich told him the milk dispenser had to be reloaded, which meant lugging the heavy refill from the cooler, hoisting it up to face level, and sliding the narrow white hose through the handle. No sooner had he finished that then he had to empty the garbage outside and rinse the cans. The line cook, first telling him to clean his hands spotless, had him peel potatoes until his thumb started to ache. By now it was time to take the ice cubes out to the waitresses stations and load the bin at the bar. He'd kept busy for two hours without washing a dish or saying hello to Maria.

His feet wet, head pounding from the noise, he stood by the Hobart, sliding in plastic trays of dishes, watching the temperature gauge steady itself at 157, and wondering how many layers of skin he'd burned and sealed at this job. If he were to touch Maria's soft cheek, she'd feel rhino hide and he'd feel nothing. In Vermont he would find a better job.

His feet still wet from the floor water, he finally sat with Maria, she with a coffee and he with a Coke. She told him about going from her counselor to a social worker. She said she was sorry she'd missed his visit on Sunday, but she'd been busy tracking people down and making arrangements to escape Steven Blanchard. "Even yesterday I left work early to—"

"I know," said Wade, "because I stopped here to have supper with you."

It won the smile he wanted to see and the pat on the hand that soothed his heart. Inside his shirt pocket he could feel the napkin, which he'd slipped into a baggie to protect it from dishwasher steam and his own sweat. No matter how tough his hand grew, he'd always feel her in the sweet package against his chest.

"I am going to leave home," she said. She spoke without slurring or sliding around it or even lowering her voice. "Whatever it takes."

In case he couldn't get to Vermont or Maria wouldn't

want to go, Wade had planned an alternative. Knowing Uncle Andrew would approve of planning made it seem almost a duty. "I found an interesting place," he said. "We could go there for a picnic tonight."

She looked at him closely, her fingers running through the dark hair by her temple. "All right. I could use a break. Only, how will I get home after?"

"I got it covered," Wade said. He felt strong. He had conquered Shawn, making the drive-in safe for Maria. He had planned this out. "Trust me."

During the dinner rush, as he pulled case after case of dishes from the stand and ran tubs of silverware through the Hobart, he foresaw a problem. By the time they got done with work, it would be dark and he'd need flashlight, food, and his cooking gear. This was no plan. This was a disaster. How was he going to get home for his equipment and get to a store for food? Not on his life would he take Maria to the apartment. When the restaurant closed, he'd still have to clean the bathrooms, sweep the dining room, and mop the kitchen. He'd have to ask Rich to let him go home for half an hour. He hated to lie to Rich, but there was no way out.

He was digging in a fry pan with steel wool when Rich tapped him on the shoulder. "How goes the schoolwork?"

For once school proved useful. He asked Rich if he could run to the library. He said he wanted to look up some World War II stuff for a test tomorrow.

"Okay, kid," Rich said, "but I want to see an A on that test."

On the way home he bought two packages of ramen noodles at Christos's, hoping Maria would like chicken flavor, and a two liter bottle of Coke. In the apartment he told his mother he had to prepare some things for school and was going right back to the restaurant. After filling two water bottles in the bathroom, he stuck them in his backpack along with the food and his cooking stuff. Knowing he'd never get the backpack past his mother, he raised his window and set the backpack outside. Then he returned to the restaurant, making it in his allotted half hour.

Rich had taken over for him, stacking dishes eight high as he pulled them out of the Hobart. He smiled at Wade and said, "You get to clean the grease trap. See, there's no such thing as free lunch."

Wade remembered he'd forgotten to punch out. Not only had he lied to Rich, he'd cheated him out of half an hour's pay. Maybe cleaning the grease trap would make up for it. Below the sink lurked the thick pipes opened only with a monkey wrench and then released, like a giant fart, Rich said, the godawful smell of baby shit. Try as they did to reclaim grease and oil, enough always escaped, so that once a month Rich told someone to clean out the trap.

As Wade scraped and dug through the stinking coagulated, congealed fat, Rich joked with him. "There's always some grease that gets by you."

The first time Wade had cleaned it, he had nearly puked. His mother told him, "It's no worse than dirty diapers." He never complained again.

There was an advantage to digging out the grease trap, particularly this night, because the rest of the crew took over the sweeping, mopping, and cleaning so that he punched out at the same time as Maria.

Lighting
a Bum

"Where're we going?" Maria asked.

Although the moon shown nearly full, he was glad he'd remembered to bring his flashlight. Hoisting the pack onto his back, he felt the handle of his sheath knife. He was glad he'd brought that too. "To the movies," he said and laughed. As they walked the near-deserted streets, he wished he could hold her hand, but just her dark-haired, pretty self smiling by his side soothed his stomach and made him feel as rested as if he'd slept all evening.

"Does your little brother's poop smell as bad as that grease trap?" he asked.

"My father's a grease trap." She stopped. Her face turned as stern as her voice. "I'm sorry, Wade, it's just that he always makes stupid jokes and noises at the table. I won't have to put up with it much longer, will I?"

"No," he said and tried to pat her hand, but it was hard to do that while they were both walking. It looked as if he were slapping at a bug.

Maria laughed as Wade played his flashlight down the long rows of speaker poles, casting shadows and cutting through the darkness like an artist with a combination brush and knife. "I've never been here before."

He explained to Maria how it wasn't hard to live on

your own if you knew how. Be exact and think ahead. Plan. Know whence you have come and whither you are going. That was the guiding wisdom he'd learned from Uncle Andrew.

"There's even an extra room," he said, shining his big light at the projection booth. "Of course this would be only temporary, in case of an emergency."

In her apartment she had her own room, and he would give her no less than what her jerk of a father provided. He'd be a good provider. His mother had told him the one thing a man must do is provide for his family.

He had borrowed a spoon from the restaurant, which he hoped Maria wouldn't notice when they ate. He owned only one spoon, bought at the Hawkeye Store, where he bought his ammo. He wasn't going to swipe one of his mother's spoons, that was for sure. He'd have to buy a spoon for Maria, though. He'd have to be prepared. He'd have to get another bowl too so he wouldn't wind up eating out of the pot like a cannibal.

"Always be ready for whatever comes along," Uncle Andrew used to say, "then you won't miss it. You won't pack your coffin with regrets." After the accident Uncle Andrew had said he was glad he'd ridden his Ninja as much as he had because now that he couldn't ride, he didn't dwell on missed opportunities. You never know when you'll run out of luck. Wade didn't believe his father was ever ready for luck. Any kind of luck, good or bad, would take his father by surprise.

From inside the concession stand came a wavering light. No electricity, no bulbs in there to turn on, the glare too bright for a flashlight. Then a shrieking screaming roared as the light moved and grew brighter. Maria grabbed Wade's arm as he swung his backpack from his shoulder. She fell. He yanked out his six inch sheath knife.

From the moving light, bellowing pounded like a giant's panicked breath. The tipped and twisted door glowed. Out ran Herman, his feet burning, hands waving, legs stumbling, yelling a monster's fearful curse. Half a foot taller than Wade, fifty pounds heavier, Herman, hideously aflame, bore down on him. Wade tackled him.

Herman screamed. Quickly he screamed again, muffled, smothered. Wade saw Maria lying on Herman's legs. She had thrown her body over him. The flame was out. Herman struggled, lunged up, and shook them both off. He screamed a cry that cut the oily air and ran off.

The moon caught Maria's face in a full mouth smile. A streak of soot marred her white jacket. From inside the concession stand, laughter. Wade checked his knife. Something stained the blade, wet and slick, sticky blood.

"I must have cut him," he said.

"Who's that?"

"Herman."

"No, in there."

This time the laughter, sharp and sour, bit into the

night's bright air like rat's teeth. Framed in the crooked doorway stood Shawn Burns. From his pocket he pulled his lighter and lit it. "For my next trick," he said. He waved fingers of his left hand over the flame. They caught fire. He raised them. "The Statue of Liberty!" He stuck the flaming fingers in his mouth to snuff them.

"You're disgusting," Maria said.

Shawn grinned. "Just dipped them in grain alcohol."

"What you did to poor Herman," Maria said.

"Spontaneous combustion." Shawn yelled, "Sooey, bum! Sooey!"

Wade felt all the strings in his body draw tight and pull from the center of his belly. Right now he could run to Shawn and rip him up the belly, unzip him before he said any more bullshit to Maria.

"Shut up," Wade said.

Shawn laughed, then ran off into the shadowy wasteland behind the burned screen.

"We should leave," Maria said.

Sheathing his knife, Wade imagined it sliding into Shawn's soft gut. But what would be the good? Shawn was no threat to him. He saw Maria already walking away in the white moonlight. "I thought Herman was attacking you," he said. Maria kept walking.

As they passed the overgrown drive-in marquee, a Rumford squad car pulled up beside them, the spotlight shining in their faces. "One of you kids carrying a big knife?" Before Wade could think how to hide his knife, the spotlight went out. "Maria Blanchard, is that you?"

"Sergeant Gallagher?"

A square-built, medium height cop got out of the car, smiled, and lit a cigarette. He leaned against the door, crossed his feet, and looked over at the drive-in sign. "Nothing playing tonight, is there?"

"We were just now startled out of our wits, Sergeant Gallagher," Maria said. "We don't need to be teased."

"Not half so scared as poor old Herman."

Herman, screaming and yelling, had called the police about two kids stabbing him with a big knife, setting his boots on fire, and trying to rob him. Sergeant Gallagher, the youth officer, had driven down to figure out the situation. "I know you didn't light him."

Maria explained that Wade had accidentally cut Herman when he tackled him. Wade said Maria had put out the fire. Neither of them mentioned Shawn Burns.

"Let me see the knife," Sergeant Gallagher said. When Wade showed it to him, the cop said, "Just a tip—this could qualify as a concealed weapon, so be sure you wear it outside your clothing."

"I didn't want to scare anybody," Wade said.

Sergeant Gallagher laughed. "So who lit old Herman?"

This wasn't Slim Jim swearing and threatening him. Besides, what did he owe that jerk, Shawn Burns? But if he told, Shawn would know. He would come after Maria.

Maybe Wade should have cut Shawn, put the fear of pain in him so he wouldn't bother them. He waited for Maria to say something.

"He ran off, Sergeant Gallagher," she said.

"Just one kid?"

"Yes," Maria said.

"He's scum," Sergeant Gallagher said. "What you two did was admirable. For what he did, he should be locked up." He waited for them to give him a name, stared at the empty moon, then with a short puff of smoke, faced them with a smile.

"You'll do us and old Herman another favor if you tell kids to leave Herman alone." He slipped his nightstick from his belt and tapped his palm with it, not so hard as to knock away his cigarette. "That's about all Herman has between him and being robbed, set afire, or generally bothered. He's sixty years old, paranoid, and he doesn't need his delusions fed by kids who think he's hid a lot of money in that cart, which he hasn't, or by kids who want to torment him." As he dragged on his cigarette, he looked up at the sign. "You have a name to give me."

"You could catch him if you drove in there now," Maria said.

"Herman can be a disagreeable old coot, but we keep an eye on him so he doesn't get hurt, or hurt someone else. He would swing that big flashlight of his on you if you cornered him."

"Like anybody," Wade said. Even Herman had to play along.

"We've got to go," Maria said, as much to Wade as to Sergeant Gallagher.

"And I've got to catch Mr. I-Don't-Know-His-Name," Sergeant Gallagher said. "Remember, if he hurt Herman, he could hurt you."

The cab fare out to The Mills cost the last ten dollars of the money Wade had taken from his mother. Though he'd be broke until payday, sitting in the cab with Maria made him pleased to have spent the money. He told her he was sorry they didn't have a good time.

"You protected me," she said.

"And you saved Herman." With his cab fare money in his hand, he felt at ease, even if he didn't have his arm around Maria. She sat on other side of the seat, by the door, too far away anyway. He asked her if things were any better at home.

"My stepmother makes this Franco-American canned spaghetti? It's easy to plop two cans into a pot, though she forgets to stir it, so I hurry it out into a bowl before it sticks and burns. My father tells me to serve his too because I'm 'a lazy fucking bitch.'" In Maria's voice neither snarl nor loudness revealed anger, nor did her face show hatred in the dull light of the cab.

"My stepmother never says a word, just starts feeding my brother that syrupy sweet, tomato-sauced pasta.

I'm thinking I could cook something different when my stepmother says this stuff is good for the baby. 'Good for me, too,' says my father, then he stuffs his mouth, puckers his lips, and squeezes his cheeks so the food spatters back into the big bowl. 'Just like baby shit,' he says. I push the bowl away, and he grabs it. 'You tight assed little twat!' I thought he was going to push my face right into the bowl and smother me. Instead he stuffed himself with another mouthful and sprayed it all over me."

Wade was as stunned by her father's language as by his actions. His mother, mean as she got, never talked like that. He was taken aback that Maria would even repeat it. Still, her father's action made him sound like a wimp. Probably like Herman, he was all bluff.

"He thought this farting noise he made was so funny," said Maria. "Juvenile, just juvenile. I feel sorry that my little brother's going to grow up with that for a father."

At her place Wade asked the driver to wait for him.

"Are you paying me another fare?" the driver asked.

Wade shook his head.

"It's another fare to take you somewhere else."

"Back to the cabstand?" Wade said quickly, not wanting Maria to find out he'd spent all his money.

"Hurry up," the driver told him.

When they reached her apartment, Maria told Wade to be prepared. As she opened her door, her father, now wearing a bright white tee-shirt, said, "Where have you been?"

"I told you I was going with Wade."

He yanked her into the apartment, then turned to Wade. "I've got ways to find out about you."

Wade, hand twitching for his knife, stood in the empty hallway. About to knock on the door, he remembered the cab driver telling him to hurry. When he got to the street, the taxi was gone. He kicked at something on the sidewalk, his backpack. At least the driver hadn't stolen it.

Walking down the strip, past the closed restaurants, mini-malls, and gas stations, Wade decided he hadn't foreseen deep enough into people. He remembered he'd promised Rich he'd ace the *Need To Be Free* test tomorrow, and soon the vicious lights around the prison hurt his eyes, so he lowered his head and trudged on. At home he was too tired to study anything. At least his mother wasn't awake to rag on him. He could count himself lucky for that.

He wasn't about to give up. Even poor old Herman, if driven into a corner, would yell and holler and swing his flashlight at you. Wade, hunter that he was, would not give up. He'd get himself out of this place, take Maria with him, and help Uncle Andrew as well. Planning and courage were things he could hold onto. Besides, he was doing right, wasn't he?

Needing
To Be
Free

"First thing is, I'm going to know where you are, and that's that." A cup of coffee in front of her face, Wade's mother peered at him as if he'd already spoiled her whole day.

This wouldn't be the end of it, Wade decided. "I'm going to school to ace that test for Rich today," he said.

"Rich puts up with you. Me, I'd've fired your butt by now."

"Got a lifetime to work, Wade," his father said. He dug his veiny fingers into Wade's collarbone. "And it don't get better." His laugh sounded hollow, like Shawn Burns' laugh in the cold cinder block space of the drive-in. Wade shrugged out of his father's painful grasp.

"We know yours isn't going to get any better," Wade's mother told his father, "and that's that."

"The dealership sends the mechanics to school down in Framingham," his father said. "I'm hoping they'll offer me the chance to go."

"Be realistic for once in your life," his mother said. "They're not going to send the test driver to school, and I wouldn't pay for it if they did."

As his mother dazed his father with arguments about lost overtime and questioned who'd pay for room and board, Wade left for school. He wanted to talk with

Maria, but with his name on the principal's list, he knew he'd better first go to the office to see Mr. Greenberg. Still hoping to see Maria, Wade made his way through a group of sophomores, noisy jays, brash and obvious. The school still proudly wore its new clothes, carpets installed last summer and a fresh coat of paint. If Wade looked long down the corridor, the vertically mounted oak beams gave the ceiling the appearance of smooth, varnished wood, but Wade raised his eyes directly overhead and saw all the conduits for air and water and electricity, pipes and wires painted a dull brown. No optical illusion fooled him because he knew enough to look up close. What hovered above your head, he believed to be far more complex than most people could admit.

At the main office door he inspected the territory. Just beyond the entrance three jean-jacketed boys, buzzards, slouched in the L-shaped row of plastic chairs. They sat close to the principal's office as if they had seniority. Wade hoped they were serving office detention because if they too were on the principal's list, he'd wait all period to see Mr. Greenberg. A shy looking, skinny girl and a preppy couple, seniors complaining that some dweeb had mistakenly put their names on the list, left an open seat between themselves and the three buzzards. Wade took the empty chair.

As the warning bell rang, the secretary in her English accent told the buzzards they could leave for class.

"Groovy," one of them said.

"Watch your mouth," said Mr. Greenberg, who had just emerged from his office. He squared his boxy shoulders and held out a thick and hairy forearm as if he might cuff the boy. "You don't want to spend all your mornings here, do you?"

"We'll bring you a doughnut," one of the other buzzards said.

"Bring me the doughnut without the detention," Mr. Greenberg told them. He raised his arm quickly, as if he might flip them off, then turned his hand to beckon Wade into his office. Wade recognized it as a kind of irony he used on students, a humor to soften the difficulties he steered them through.

Wade, sitting in an armless chair, felt open to attack even though Mr. Greenberg wheeled his chair out from behind his desk. In fact, facing Mr. Greenberg with no desk between them made things too exposed for Wade. He pulled his hands from his lap to let them dangle like weights. He felt like a betrayer.

"What is this you delivered to me?" Mr. Greenberg asked. "Junk mail?"

From his desk he yanked a WITHDRAWAL FROM SCHOOL form and scaled it into Wade's lap. The paper, smudged with the erasable ink Wade had used, looked as if it had been filled out by some grammar school kid. Wade's face burned fuzzy red.

Mr. Greenberg leaned forward. "You know, in Boston you see these guys down on their luck handing out promos for everything from massage parlors to the Church of the Holy Ghost on Wheels." Mr. Greenberg pointed his heavy eyebrows at Wade. "Passing them over without a smile or a tear, just like you with this form."

"You go to church, Mr. Greenberg?" Wade thought of Uncle Andrew in the church he longed to go back to.

"First off, Wade, I'm a Jew. We go to synagogue. You never see an ad for a synagogue or itinerant rabbis stuck under your wiper blade. When Jews go crazy, they become Christians." He laughed.

Wade wanted to laugh with him, but he didn't think he could smile, even if he were getting cash by the minute for it. "I am the lighter of the world," Wade said.

"Are you religious, Wade? I hope I didn't offend you."

"I guess even God must need clowns." Wade's hands flew to his face.

"Are you clowning around with this withdrawal form?"

Wade could see that his mother's forged permission signature looked like all the rest of his writing on the form.

Mr. Greenberg explained how students wove webs for themselves, silk strands of contingencies that covered their eyes and blurred their vision. But sometimes this blindness could keep kids from doing something really stupid. Nowhere in his talk were the accusations, the blame, the condemnation Wade's mother always sauced her speeches with. Even with his sarcasm, Mr. Greenberg sounded more like Uncle Andrew than like Wade's mother. As if he were a doctor peering into an open mouth, Mr. Greenberg spread Wade's file folder with thumb and forefinger.

He started reading its contents out loud. Reports of skipped classes. Reports of detentions attended. No skipped detentions. No fights—wait, one fight, Wade not at fault. One drug incident, last year. That was the time Wade and John had taken apart a lot of Tylenol capsules, put the granules into plastic baggies, and taken them to school in a paper bag. In the smoking area they'd bragged about making profits enough to fly out of Rumford. Their boasting had provoked a teacher who had overheard them to turn them in along with their stash.

"Did you think you could get high on that stuff?" Mr. Greenberg asked. "Did you confuse it with Contac?"

"It was only a joke." Wade looked at his feet and laughed. Once he and John had tried separating out the "good parts" of Contac. He'd ended up with a face burning red, as if his face wasn't already bad enough, a new zit every day to betray him, his body a constant catastrophe.

"About taking off from school yesterday."

"I was sick," Wade said.

"Not so sick that you couldn't go down to the drive-in last night."

"How'd you—"

"Sergeant Gallagher called this morning to check up

on you. I told him if you were with Maria Blanchard, you weren't lighting any of the homeless."

"I was trying to sort out some problems," Wade said. "I do get gut aches. I wasn't lying about being sick."

"Some problems you don't lie your way out of. You see your guidance counselor." Mr. Greenberg didn't ask Wade if Maria were his girlfriend, though it was obvious he approved of Maria. Maybe that was why he was going easy on Wade. "You have to sign out when you go home early from school, Wade; otherwise, it's a skip, classes cut."

"I'll serve the detentions, Mr. Greenberg. I'll start today."

"Don't make trouble for yourself, Wade. You don't need spiders crawling all over your face." Mr. Greenberg shoved the WITHDRAWAL FORM back in Wade's file like a weak chick he'd decided not to cull. "The bum last night, Herman, didn't know the kid who torched him. You tell me who it was."

If it were just Wade and Shawn, Wade would speak out, face to face, and call him a sadistic creep. But ratting on him was betrayal. And Shawn could find sneaky ways to hurt Maria. Besides, they'd make Wade stay in Rumford to testify against Shawn. He couldn't do that. Time had dragged his face down until his chin felt weighted and his jaw muscles clenched.

"I didn't recognize him," he said. "I didn't see him real clear." He hated denying the accuracy with which he saw things.

Mr. Greenberg let the room heat and draw close, like that cell in the Edgar Allen Poe story. Time toyed cruelly with Wade, laying out a silence into which he could not laugh.

"Mr. Greenberg, if you go to another school—" Wade hesitated, his hand hid his face, then he found the trail again. "Say you move, do you have to fill out that form?"

"Usually. Sometimes kids move over the summer, then the new school sends for their transcripts. Course if this is you, Wade, there's a note here that says you're on probation. You'd need written permission from your probation officer to move."

"Even if it were out of state?"

"Your probation officer might not let you move out of state."

"It's not me," Wade said. He knew Maria would want to go to school once they got to Vermont.

"You can't quit at all without permission from your p.o."

"I'm here now."

"Don't go crazy on me, Wade."

He wasn't on probation. Last year when he'd gone to Mr. Greenberg for class cuts, he'd said he'd been charged with assault for fighting a gang of kids who had picked on John. He'd claimed he'd ended up on probation until he was eighteen. Actually, he'd wanted to see Mr. Greenberg's reaction, goof on him and see if he would reveal himself in a laugh or an absurd comment. Now it was in Wade's file. Now he had a record. Just as he had told Maria. He should laugh. Wade could use a big laugh right now.

Blue card in hand, Wade trudged out of the office, through the door to the stairway, then back up to his third floor social studies class. He'd like to go down to the caf for some chocolate milk, maybe spot Maria in her English class, but Mr. Greenberg, as he always did, had written the time Wade had left on the blue card. Some kids, when teachers asked for their blue cards, just yanked the tip out of their pocket, showing only the color. Wade wasn't about to trust to luck. Not this close to Vermont, this close to Maria.

As he entered the classroom, he held out his palm, bearing the blue card like an offering. Sure enough, Mac, the teacher, inspected it. Wade was glad he hadn't lied to Mac, who'd always treated him fairly. There were so few chances to find Maria, though, that Wade felt trapped by his own honesty.

In the back of the room sat Peter with Shawn Burns. Peter, smiling, nodded to an empty chair in front of him. To show he wasn't afraid of Shawn, Wade took it. Mac was talking about slogans, whether from televisions ads, movies, or songs, and kids called out examples, which Mac wrote on the board. Peter, laboriously, copied them into his notebook. Neither Shawn nor Wade had a notebook.

Wade knew that didn't make them alike.

"This sucks," Shawn said.

Suddenly the class was quiet. "Explain," Mac told him.

"I was just wondering where that slogan came from," Shawn said. "The gay community?"

Groans and laughter answered him. Mac held silent for a moment then said, "Cursing and vulgarity have always been part of American discourse. You didn't think you invented swearing, did you, Shawn?"

"If I had, I'd be collecting a lot of royalties around this place."

Wade had failed a social studies class last year for too many absences, which was why he had to take *You and the Law* on top of Mac's class. Shawn and Peter were in that section too. Shawn needed an easy credit, Peter liked the field trips. He said in a couple of days they were going to the county courthouse to watch a trial. He showed Wade a half grin that made him look like his face was paralyzed. Wade thought of Uncle Andrew, smiling despite his paralysis.

In Mr. B's English class Wade answered all the test questions about *The Need To Be Free*. He had read all the selections, from a piece on the Cherokee Trail of Tears to stories about the Japanese internment camps in World War II, anti-Semitism during the Depression, poverty, mental illness, and prisons. Knowing how easily he understood them, he was sure he had an *A*.

On the board, next to the daily quote, Mr. B wrote a short essay topic. Every time Mr. B gave a test, the quote was "Stay Cool." Peter said there was something like that in *The Hitchhikers Guide to the Galaxy*. Peter had offered to lend Wade his copy, but Wade didn't like to borrow books or anything else.

ESSAY TOPIC FOR THE NEED TO BE FREE

This unit has explored different concepts of freedom. Briefly describe your concept of freedom. Try to give specific examples of what you mean.

At the top of his paper Wade wrote "When you're on your own, you're free." It was close to the quote Mr. B had put on the board the day they'd started reading this unit. Though he couldn't remember the author, he knew it was from a song. Mr. B often quoted song lyrics, usually old ones. Wade wondered if Mr. B and Mac ever got together to talk about old music, like the Beatles or the Stones.

There was never any music in Wade's house because his mother liked it quiet, quiet as a tomb, she'd say. When she watched television, she pulled her chair up close and turned the volume real low, as if she didn't want to share her show.

Writing, half in printing, half in cursive, Wade started his essay.

When some people notice that others are not like them, then they think that the other people are lower and not equal to who those people are. Then they decide to pick on them and make their lives miserable, not even knowing how other people feel.

Wade thought about how upperclassmen picked on sophomores and how Slim Jim had picked on him and Ernie, how his mother ragged on him. He had plenty of examples. He could even write down about Maria's father, but he didn't. He wrote about the Cherokees, the Japanese, and the Jews. He wondered if being Jewish made Mr. Greenberg more understanding of kids in trouble.

I would like the world that surrounds us to be free of all the little catches that go with everything. The small print always takes away the promise of the big print. Like a teacher saying I would have given you an A for this paper if you'd used blue ink. Like not getting credit for the books I read because they weren't on the approved reading list.

I want to be free from consciousness of what other people think, free of worrying about it. I want not to be my own worst enemy.

Why did he write that? He looked around to be sure no one saw it. During the test Mr. B walked around to help and give hints and see how they were doing. Mr. B stood practically right behind him. Slowly, with no big show, Wade drew lines through that last sentence. What a dumb thing to write. As if he didn't know who his enemies were.

If I wanted to live free, I would move deep into the country, buy hundreds of acres of land, and build myself a home with a brook or pond next to it. There would be a little country store, but the nearest supermarket would be two hours away. The only people around me would be those who needed my help.

That's enough, Wade thought. He didn't have to write

about Vermont or Uncle Andrew directly, certainly not about Maria. Mr. B was a nice enough teacher, but he probably thought Wade would wind up a scuffle-butt drifter chasing a rusty rainbow, just another Herman pushing his shopping cart through the woods.

As he was about to turn in his test, the stomp of marching feet and cadenced, indecipherable calling came into the classroom. At first a couple of kids from the side, then the whole class, clustered at the windows. Below in the upper parking lot tramped the perennially victorious field hockey team, waving sticks as they left for a distant game. All preps, all used to winning, they would one day soon leave Rumford for college, which they saw as another kind of winning. And so it is, Wade thought, only I'll be leaving soon too. It'll be my victory, and I won't need it announced over the loudspeaker.

Little Connie with her short hair and tight yellow Speedway t-shirt yelled out the window. "Snobs!"

"Sit down," Mr. B said, "and stop yelling."

"They are snobs," said Jim.

"Even if they are, you have a test to finish."

"I'm done," Wade said.

"Me, too," Jim said.

But Mr. B saw that Jim had written no essay and told him he needed those points. Connie said Wade had written his essay. She held up his paper. "He wants to be a hermit and deprive us of his company."

"At least he won't have to listen to a damned marching field hockey team," Jim said.

Everybody laughed, even Mr. B.

Wade belonged to no team, only to himself. Since he had come to Rumford, he'd been on his own, but now he had family (Uncle Andrew) and a friend (Maria), which didn't make up a clique. John liked football, so it was okay for him to be on a team. It didn't turn him into a snob. Peter accepted everybody, which was why he sat with Shawn Burns. Then there was Riley, tough talking Riley, who lived with his father because his mother's house was too noisy, ("Chaos, man, it's chaos over there," he'd told Wade.) He always had an answer for everything, but his insides, Wade thought, trapped a loneliness as desperate as any Wade knew. Riley was too regular to know how much luck he needed.

Maria, with her soft eyes and chocolate sauce spotted chin, didn't seem lonely or part of a team, and she was separating from her family. Just talking to Maria made his gut pains stop, at least made him stop thinking about them. He'd told her his mother sucked things into her nasty maw and soaked them in her digestive juices until their bones dissolved, as his father's had. You weren't supposed to say stuff about your own mother, but Wade had said it, had told Maria, and the earth hadn't opened up. Instead, he'd felt better. He felt better than he had in a long time.

As Mr. B was collecting the tests, a voice from

the loudspeaker reminded all juniors to report to the auditorium for an assembly next period. That would mean Wade couldn't see Maria in the caf.

"What's that about?" Jim asked.

"Scheduling for next year," Mr. B said, "when most of you will be seniors." He shook the sheaf of test papers at Jim.

Down a flight amid juniors saying, "No fucking French. No goddamn math. Yeah, and no chance for a cigarette," Wade looked for Maria. He didn't care about scheduling for next year because by next week he'd be in Vermont.

He entered the auditorium balcony, where the film classes met, where last year he had sat with Peter to watch a three hour videotape of *The Seven Samurai*. Peter had convinced him that if Mr. B said it was a great film, they would like it. Wade had liked it. Now he sat with four hundred juniors and tried to spot Maria. Mr. Greenberg grabbed the mike as confidently as he might pick up a small dog. The kids quieted.

"Last year," Mr. Greenberg began, "you were sophomores, toads along the academic garden path. Now you are juniors, but next year you will be mighty seniors." A roar accompanied by shrieks and whistles interrupted him. "It will be time to hop on out of here. But I'm on this stage to tell you a sad fact of life. THERE IS NO GRADUATION FAIRY!"

Where was Maria? Twisting, turning, Wade scanned

the balcony but could not find her while Mr. Greenberg, not offering many funny remarks now, talked about the importance of scheduling in order to get in all the required classes. There she was on the main floor near the stage. Her dark hair curled up, her arm spread jauntily on the seat back next to her. As a hunter, Wade could identify his target from this easy distance every time. Staring at the back of her head, he was so sure the girl he focused on was Maria that he willed her to turn and look at him.

As the guidance counselor introduced by Greenberg droned on about graduation requirements, Wade looked straight out, over the heads of his classmates, into the open space of the auditorium. Five skinny white pipes for the sprinkler system crossed the auditorium ceiling. From the far right pipe dangled a pink balloon maybe twenty feet from the floor, probably left over from some silly celebration. Nearer to Wade, a chandelier hung from the ceiling, a circle mounted by points like a lighted crown. He could leap from the bottom of the balcony, grab the chandelier, and hang from the lighted crown.

Imagining meant he could fly. Flying raised him above everything ordinary. It raised him above all the rah-rahs, all the petty, two-bit heroes of the high school: the brown-nosers, the jocks, the preps, all the pretty boys on parade, the field hockey team, all the stuck-up girls. They couldn't fly. They didn't even imagine flying. The games of winning and losing, grades and honors, kept them from seeing what hovered just over their heads.

Wade bet he was the only kid in the auditorium who imagined flying. That's what made him different from all the others. None of them would appreciate it if he flew to the chandelier unless he fell. Ten for style, some jerk would say.

He wished Maria would turn and look at him. It was the whole point of going to this assembly, and she never even saw him. Maybe she'd looked while he mind-flew out to the chandelier.

When the assembly let out, Wade merged with the crowd and hoped to meet Maria in the downstairs foyer. Clumps of students rose from the main floor, jamming the stairway. At the first floor he hurried from the stairway to the corridor and to the left, only to find the auditorium foyer empty. Looking right, he saw halfway down the corridor the dark, upturned hair.

He decided she had headed for the library. Like the hunter he was, he figured an alternate route: hike down to the basement floor, speed across the nearly empty hallway, cut over to the vocational wing and trudge up the ramp to the library's side entrance. Although a bunch of students had gathered at the library door, none of them was Maria. He decided he had beaten her there. He waited inside, his copy of *Night Shift* propped in front of him as he inspected the table's wood surface.

Around the edge ran pale oak arrows. Shifting his

position slightly he aimed his table arrows at the preppy couple who giggled on the dark brown couch backed against a square white pillar. They sat playing little finger games, confident, as if their parents had bought the couch just for them. The swish of drawers sliding in and out of the card catalogue drew Wade's attention. A tall sophomore winked to his buddy as he ran the drawer suggestively in and out. They think they're daring rebels, he told himself, and the preps think they own the place. With a good hunting bow, he could end their smugness, show them their darkness.

Back in Newfound Ernie had bought real hunting arrows with money he'd gotten for his twelfth birthday. Ernie's parents had given him a sportsman's bow with a fifty pound pull, and his brother had bought him shooting gloves to keep his fingers from getting bruised. "This bow," Ernie told Wade, "will give you a twang."

Up at the old sandpits Wade waited for Ernie. The bright morning sun of early June dried the yellow particles and set them sparkling. From the top of the hill he looked over the town. Shading his eyes with his hand, he scanned the trails that led down to the railroad tracks, the juncture of the rivers, the main street. He didn't spot anyone sneaking up. Ernie, of course, would come from behind, up the old Indian trail, silent as an Indian scout. The previous year for his fifth grade class Wade had drawn a big map of Newfound with all the Indian trails and their grinding stone on the hill and their corn fields, shown in neatly penciled shapes shaded with special crayons the teacher had loaned him. The teacher had said it was the best she had ever seen and asked him if he wanted to be an archeologist. He'd told her he wanted to be an Indian.

Balance lost, arms flailing, Wade fell into dry particles of gold that pushed into his face and rushed up his shirt. Two white men had jumped him and shoved his face into the loose sand. Denny and Jay, ninth graders. "You're going to die, you little fuck," Denny said.

"Yeah, Rule," Jay said, "we don't let no assholes up here. This is ours."

Wade shut up. They would kill him, but he'd die as silently as a Mohawk brave. Denny stepped on his neck. The rubber of his sneaker smelled like cigarette butts as it jammed his face into the sand. Sand in his mouth, he heard Jay laughing. "You're going to choke on sand." Jay laughing, Denny laughing, laughing, then screaming, crying. The sneaker off his face, Wade saw Jay with an arrow in his thigh, Denny backing away, trying not to fall, afraid to turn. Ernie aimed another arrow at Denny. Jay screamed as he pulled the metal hunting point from his leg. He jolted lamely down the sand hill trying to catch up with Denny.

In the library a girl sat on the floor between two rows of books, her white skirt flared around her like the petals of a strange flower. When she turned a page, she glanced at Wade, saw his book, smiled, then shifted her body slightly as she returned to reading. The carpet fascinated Wade. Off to the side, a sea of orange floated other tables, islands a yard square. But under his feet the sea revealed its threads as red, mostly red, and yellow and brown. So what happened? What happened when you got off in the sea, far enough away? You weren't red, brown, or yellow. You melted in orange, burnt orange, they called it, not knowing what it was to burn a color.

The flower petal girl wore her dark hair turned up, like Maria's. Maybe he'd mistaken her for Maria back in the hallway. He shouldn't sit here staring at this girl when he could be out looking for Maria. At least he could look for Riley to set up their ride to Vermont. Riley, when he wasn't in class, hung out in the smoking area just outside the caf. Riley held to his habits. He had no surprises.

Rattlesnake
Hill

Walking down the stairs to the smoking area, Wade didn't see Riley, but his eagle eye caught Maria sitting at one of the cafeteria tables, eating her lunch alone. He sat across from her, too full of talk to be hungry.

Wade told Maria about the Newfound sandpit, only he said he had shot Jay with the hunting arrow, which was true in a way because he would have shot Jay. Dangerous as lynx, Denny and Jay didn't just threaten, they blackened your eyes, knocked out your teeth, broke your bones. With someone like that, you had to hurt them. He wondered if he should have hurt Shawn Burns, then Shawn wouldn't have torched Herman. In Newfound things had been so simple that you always knew what to do. "The simple truth," his mother always demanded. "All I want is the simple truth, and all I get is lies."

He told Maria the library's burnt orange carpet reminded him of his mother.

"Your mother?"

One Saturday back in Newfound his mother had made candy on the stove. Caramel flowed from ladle to pot, a river of pale brown. She asked his father to watch it while she walked downtown for groceries. His father fell asleep on the divan. The ashy smell of burning candy stung

Wade's eyes. When his mother returned, he complained that the candy hurt him. Smack in his face came the ladle. His mother, yelling words he hadn't understood, smacked him again. The next morning Wade found the candy, brittle and black, in the garbage. He bit it, tasted it, and swallowed it before his tongue had been able to stop him. Burnt was bad, he discovered.

He'd like to burn his mother in a kettle of sticky burnt orange, candy carpet fibers that would flow down her throat and clog her lungs. He'd wait a long time before he snatched her heart. Like a true Indian. Smack me with the ladle, sting and burn, would you? I'll tear up every part of you and save your heart for last.

"I'd like to rub all the hurt out of the world," he told Maria, "but a brave has to be brave, has to hold in his feelings and act with cunning."

Maria held his hand. "I know how angry you are, but you can't let it eat at you. You have to do something."

"I'm going to find Riley," he said. "He'll take me to my uncle's in Vermont."

"That's doing something." She let go of his hand and smiled at him.

"As soon as I find out when we can leave, I'll tell you." He thought she'd touch him again, but she didn't.

"The sooner the better, I think."

He watched Maria take her tray up to the kitchen, then walk back toward her class, giving him a little wave as she passed his table. All his talk and telling stories had worn him out. Fatigue hit him as if he were being attacked with a club. Toughing out the rest of his classes made him feel like a genuine brave. He even served an hour in detention.

After detention Wade walked downtown but not to work. Neither he nor Maria was scheduled today. Tomorrow he could bring Rich the *Need To Be Free* test with his *A*. Today he would plan for his escape. Travel light, that was the trick, that and be prepared.

In Osco's he picked up a pack of Big Red, which he carried deliberately and openly in his hand as he made his way to the back of the store. As the blue-coated pharmacist fixed up fancy drugs, Wade slid a package of Trojans from the rack into his pocket. He hoped they didn't come in sizes because he hadn't examined what he was taking, just a box, $6.98. Mirrors at the end of the counter stared down at him. There were no security cameras here that he could see though he knew they sometimes hid them in the ceiling. Above him all the tiles looked whole. He knew a shoplifting charge would make them come after him.

"Something you need help with?" the pharmacist asked. From the raised platform the man looked at Wade, eyes shifting to his hands.

"I'm supposed to pick up a prescription for my mother, but I just remembered it's at Rumford Pharmacy."

"You sure? I can look it up for you."

Wade didn't want to give his name. He shook his head.

"I'm sure."

"You have the prescription? I can probably give her a better price than at Rumford."

Was this a game to force him to go into his pockets? Had the pharmacist seen him steal the condoms? Right now the package seemed as big as his sheath knife. "Can I pay for this gum here?"

Wade brought out coins that seemed to have a hard day's sweat coating them and dropped them in the pharmacist's hand. He refused a bag and walked out of the store, register slip and gum held out openly, feeling proud that he could take care of his needs in town as well as in the woods. He didn't plan to sleep with Maria, but he wanted to be prepared, as his uncle had always told him. "God requires practicality," Uncle Andrew had said, "as well as practice."

He walked to John's house and showed him the package of condoms, in case he'd stolen the wrong ones. If John said something critical, he'd just laugh and throw them out. "What d'ya get those for?" John asked. "You think you might get lucky?"

"I don't want any accidents," Wade said. He was glad John didn't laugh at him about the condoms or when he asked him to hike up Rattlesnake Hill. Dave, the football player, had told Wade about sneaking down at night to the city reservoir on the other side of Rattlesnake Hill with his father to fish for lakers and pickerel. Wade had asked Dave where the spot was so that he could take his father some night. A trail known to old Rumford families like Dave's led from an overgrown logging road to a spot hidden from the main road.

"I don't have time to fish," Wade's father had said, "especially not in the dark at the goddamn public water supply."

The great hill west of the city hid no rattlesnakes because the early quarry workers had shot all the long fat timber rattlers. Wade was curious to see such snakes, but John wasn't. He said even though he'd been up there before, the place made him nervous. Wade told him he wanted to scout it out as a place to camp because he was going to leave home soon and would need a place to live. Wade convinced John to show him the trail through the woods to the great hole where granite slabs, ridged and drilled, lay about like pieces of a megalithic temple. For a while they watched purple sky fingers try to grab the towers and wires that grew out of the granite quarry. John, unafraid to speak his fear, said a boy had died up here.

"A graduation party before you moved to Rumford. They partied here, and he left with his girlfriend way in the middle of the night without a flashlight."

This boy had slipped on the dark sloping trail, tumbling head over heels off the edge and had fallen into an abandoned quarry where rocks mashed his brains out. This history reminded Wade that years of walls, walls of accidents and ballgames and relatives, walls of birthday parties and first girlfriends, and even walls of jokes, separated him from all these Rumford kids, even friendly ones like John. It was like a catechism you learned by living through it.

"What happened to the girlfriend?" Wade asked.

"Nothing deadly," John said, "but they say she screamed so long, she lost her voice and couldn't speak a word for a year."

If Maria were to hear of Wade's death, he was sure her piercing scream would cut everyone who heard until they bled from their eyeballs. She would scream with such loyalty that her lungs would have to collapse before she stopped.

The first bad sign at the quarries was the gravel parking area churned by too many cars. The second bad sign showed up just past the gate, a huge metal bar with a counterbalance. Strangely, though the bar fit through a post with a hoop, no lock secured it. John easily lifted it. Down the narrow tar road Wade saw bright spray-painted words.

LOOK DARLENE ABBOT RIGHT THERE MARCH15 SORRY HA HA

"Maybe somebody else needed those condoms," John said.

"He shouldn't have made a big deal out of it." Unless it was big deal, it didn't count for some guys. That was too philosophical to think about right now because here came a good sign, a rutted dirt track that left the asphalt and went straight, girdling the hill.

In shadows dying into darkness stood a patch of white birch. Wade told John it would be a good place to hunt because a blow-down area beyond it had begun to turn swampy. John, city boy that he was, had thought you hunted deer on mountains or in dense pine forests until Wade explained to him about deer needing food and water.

Farther along lay the old quarries, filled with water. In the first hot days of summer kids would run sweating through trails in the woods to dive into the deep, frigid water. An industrial swimming pool, John had called it, where you swung out on the rope thirty feet above the water. Tonight might be Wade's last chance to see the quarries.

Down a side path they went through six foot poplars, dry ferns, scrub pine, more or less following a power line. Along the way were a couple of beer cans, more bad signs. Just beyond a muddy section they reached an open flat with an old foundation topped by bent rebar like the walls of some sunken fort. To the right lay a football field sized quarry, its water reflecting smooth granite and ringed with paper birch and sugar maples. On one of the lichen-covered slabs someone had spray painted: SCOTT BEAUCHESNE IS A RAT.

At least it didn't say WADE RULE, though that was

only because Wade wasn't a big deal like Scott, who had parties at his house where he could display his "meat muscle," offer "hot beef injections," and provide all the beer and dope you could want. That was the word at school, at least that was Scott's word. Wade figured not all Scott's customers were well pleased.

Crisscrossing paths of confusion took them past jumbled rock piles ten feet high, along blackberry patches, and finally brought them to the main old quarry. In the middle of the round hole floated a lobster trap buoy—someone's idea of a joke or marking a case of beer? A mess of beer cans lay next to a fire ring. Across from him in reversed silhouette letters **DEEP PURPLE** reflected from the glassy surface. Next to the distorted words a fallen, rotted birch leaned into the water, its reflection bent awkwardly in an impossible reproduction that grew up and down at the same time.

"How deep is it?" Wade asked.

"Nobody knows, but there are hidden rocks sticking up along the edge. That's why you have to drop away from the shore." John pointed to the heavy rope tied around a big oak on the cliff edge. "Swinging out on the rope is scary at first," John said, "but then you see you're going to land in water, and you can't miss. First time I did it, I was half-cocked. That icy water turns your balls into marbles. The cold shocks you more than the fall."

"I could never do that," Wade said. There were far too

many people coming and going here for him to ever call this home. They walked farther down the hill until they came to the working quarry, at least eighty feet down with no water at the bottom.

"I can jump into the water," John said, "but I'll tell you what, I couldn't climb those things." He pointed to the towering poles that supported the cables running deep into the cut slabs of granite. "You fall from one of those, you don't fall into water. You're just a stain on the rock. Guys say that's where the pink granite comes from."

Studded with metal rungs lined up like the armor plates on some dinosaur neck, the pole rose fifty feet into the darkening sky. Leaping, Wade reached the first one and, hips swiveling, climbed up and up, scaling the monster. The rusty iron rungs ran cold through his fingers. Above him the purple streaks darkened as his hands gripped and gripped and slipped. One hand, free and deadly, the other latched tight as a dog's jaws locked onto the neck of his prey. Wade hugged the pole.

John stood far down in the shadows, too far away to have seen the slip. He waved and yelled something that Wade couldn't make out. Sweat running down his wrist stained his flesh dull red—like pink granite? Fear trembles quivered through his arms and legs. He'd climbed too high. Turning from the pole and looking down, he opened his wet, shaking hand and forced a wave to John far below, a small figure on the safe ground. Wade decided he'd done enough. Stop shaking or you won't be able even to climb down. Then, almost against his own will, up he grabbed, rung, rung, next rung, hands and feet steady now, a rhythmic climbing to no beat but his own in the dangerous dark.

He wanted to hear John say, *The crazy bastard climbed all the way to the top.*

The top, empty and flat, was just the top. Wade stared down from the great height of the pole to John, who couldn't possibly understand anything Wade might yell. Wade wanted to hurry down, rushing against a prickly desire to fall, like some scab saying *pick me,* which he knew would only bleed endlessly even if it would stop itching. His wet hands told him to go slow, grab firm, don't be rushed. Not letting go with one hand before he had squeezed the next rung with the other, really squeezed in a death grip, a life grip. It staved off the desire to fall. Grip, grip, grip until letting himself drop to the ground, he could grin at John.

"Amazing, Wade," John said. "Fucking crazy."

On their way back through the woods, Wade spotted a white birch with a telltale circled rupture. "Somebody does hunt in Rumford," he told John. "Illegally too. He's salted this tree." Without waiting for John's question, he explained that setting out salt licks to attract deer was not only illegal but obvious, so some hunters ("meat hunters," he added) blew rock salt into trees with their shotgun. "At least he's staying legal by using a shotgun within the city limits, ha, ha. Off this trail he'll have made a stand," Wade said as he stepped into the woods.

"It's too dark to be fucking around in there," John said. "That's how that kid got killed, getting off the trail."

Patting the tree's smooth bark as if it were a friend, Wade rejoined John on the trail. He'd leave alone John's fears of falling into a hole like the dead boy. Wade had no need to pick on other people's scabs.

Instead of going home, Wade walked to John's mother's house where cardboard boxes covered the floors like pieces of some giant board game.

"You should've seen this dude," John announced, "climbing up that pole like he was walking down Main Street."

John's mother, a big woman with a big smile, laughed until she had to set down the box she held like a child. With a move as fast as a wind switch, Mrs. Adams grabbed Wade and clutched him to her breast. "You watch yourself, watch your feet and your face, and you'll be all right. I'd hate for any of John's friends to fall into harm." The familiar smell of beer blended in an oddly pleasant way with sweat, perfume, and cigarette smoke. She was warm with smells.

Mrs. Adams was moving to an apartment above the bar she had just leased in Manchester. Out the front door Wade, John, Mrs. Adams, and her boyfriend lugged boxes to the cube truck the boyfriend had borrowed from his job.

Gradually the floor in the house appeared, worn linoleum like the floor of Wade's house, though never so cold, never so dark. Even empty, the flat had the feel of a place where someone would turn the sheets down for him, like in his father's relatives' farmhouse. He would do that for Uncle Andrew when they lived together.

"I wish Maria were here," Wade said as they squeezed into the truck's cab. "She likes moving."

"She your girlfriend?" Mrs. Adams asked, and when Wade nodded, she said, "You'll have to bring her down to my place. I'll treat her. Course if she were here now, you two would have to ride in back with the boxes." She pinched his thigh and laughed like air rushing into a closed room. She kept him laughing nearly the whole twenty minute ride.

When they reached Manchester, John's older sister Jen and her boyfriend joined them in carrying boxes up the wide stairs to the apartment above the bar. They filled the living room, covering its bare wood floors.

"I always wanted wood floors," Mrs. Adams said. "These will wax up like the gleam in a lover's eye. Right, Wade?" She ruffled his hair.

No one, not even Ms. Plizak, ruffled his hair or pinched him, or joked about his girlfriend. It came so fast he didn't have time to do anything but enjoy it. Would Maria ruffle his hair one day?

"What kind of floors in your place?" Mrs. Adams

asked.

"Carpet in the living room," Wade said. "My mother says she likes rugs because they don't show dirt."

"Time for a beer and a smoke," Mrs. Adams said.

They trooped down narrow stairs to the back of the closed bar as quietly as if they were breaking into the place. Mrs. Adams' boyfriend pulled cans from their plastic rings and slid them down the long wooden table as if he were bowling strikes. Wade ignored his beer, and Mrs. Adams replaced it with a Coke. Wade wondered if Mrs. Adams had chosen the club because of all the wood: floors, tables, even knotty pine paneling on the walls.

"Next time we'll have the grill going so we can feed everybody," Mrs. Adams said. "You'll bring your girlfriend for that, won't you, Wade? We want to meet the little hussy that would take a sweet thing like you out of circulation."

"She's going to move to Vermont," Wade said.

"Hey," John said, "you should have seen this dude climb the pole up at the quarry. He scaled all the way to the top."

At home Wade's mother sat at the kitchen table waving her cigarette like a magic wand. Her hair stuck out over her ears so wildly Wade thought a wisp might catch fire from her cigarette.

"Some friends you got," she said.

She complained about how late it was and how he

hadn't called to let her know where he was. Her words weaved through the smoke, darting and stinging, allowing only half sentences from him to explain the evening. Naturally, he didn't tell her about climbing the quarry tower. She said she knew he was lying to her because he was allergic to the simple truth. She ended by telling him she'd cashed his paycheck.

He'd forgotten it was payday. "Where's my money?"

"If that's the kind of family John comes from, keeping you out to all hours and taking you to a bar, you'd just better stay away from him."

"Where's my money?" Right now he could reach across the table to throttle her, digging his fingers into her throat until he tore out the filthy, wailing vocal cords. "I want my pay. I worked for it, I earned it."

"I needed it for the rent."

"Liar!"

"Don't call me what you are, Wade. I know what you are. Don't you ever forget that. I know exactly what you are."

A Sign

Bitter coffee odor and tobacco smoke invaded Wade's bedroom and crammed down his throat as though Jay and Denny had forced him to eat his way through the ashes in the firepit at the quarries. Someday he'd like to go back to Newfound, join up with Ernie, and track down Jay and Denny. You made me eat sand, but you were the ones who ran away. He didn't want to hurt them; just reminding them of what happened would satisfy him. Didn't Uncle Andrew say God made man eat dust, except those lucky enough to taste venison?

Wade had eliminated the drive-in and the quarries as possible camps. His mother wouldn't leave his money lying around like eggs in a nest for him to take. He had to talk this out with Maria, sweet Maria, whose very listening calmed him. He swore if he ate sand and dirt and ashes too while she were with him, his mouth would taste pure and his stomach wouldn't hurt. Maybe that was why love was a miracle. Right now gut pains wracked him, but he wouldn't complain. The last time he'd told his mother his stomach hurt, she'd asked him if he needed an enema.

"What are these?" Standing, holding the red and white box, she looked like some spirit risen from the ground. A wreath of smoke clouded her head as she shook the box at him.

"Those aren't mine," Wade said, thinking of the Trojans in her bedroom.

"You stole them?"

Gotcha! What could he say? He couldn't even explain to her why he'd taken them from Osco's. He wanted to pull the blanket over his head and wait in the dark until she went away, but she wouldn't go away. She'd yank the covers right off him.

"Those don't always work, you know." She held out the box as if she might make him put one on. "You think they're magic? You have one, she won't get pregnant, but she'll get pregnant all right. Then who's going to pay the bills? You?"

"I won't get anyone pregnant," he said.

"I'm going to sit down with Maria and tell her about how she'll get pregnant. How it isn't even an accident, it's negligence on the part of the man, only when the man in question is a boy like you who can't tell the truth even about a simple thing—"

"I don't lie!" Damn her, she took his money, now she wanted to take his girlfriend.

"You lied to Rich just the other night, telling him you were going to the library when you came right here. He even took over for you himself. I'd be surprised if he doesn't fire you."

"How will he know?"

"I told him. You don't catch me lying. I'm no hypocrite."

"I got an A on that test, and I'll bring it to Rich today."

"I thought you were quitting school, or was that just another lie?"

On the way to school he wondered if she'd remember to take the Trojans out of her pocket. He'd love to see a crack in her smugness. He'd love to be at the restaurant when she pulled her checks from her pocket and out flew the red and white Trojan box. He could see it land right on a customer's dessert plate. How'd she like to be standing there embarrassed and stammering, trying to figure out a way to recoup her tip?

In first period Shawn Burns teased Peter about their field trip to the courthouse tomorrow for *You and The Law*. "Maybe we'll see someone hung," he said. "You could see me hung if you got down on your knees."

"When does it leave?" Wade asked. If the field trip would make him miss seeing Maria during their free period, he'd skip it.

"Right after this period," Peter said.

Wade wanted to leave for Vermont as soon as possible. Only now he had no money, Rich might fire him, and Uncle Andrew wouldn't know he was coming. He wished for a sign. If Rich did fire him, he could ask for the pay they held back—what was it? Three or four days' worth? He could grab that without his mother horning in.

If he made it over the border to Uncle Andrew's before

his mother knew what was going on, she wouldn't spend time and energy to bring him back with the complications of state lines and all, at least if he didn't break any laws. She couldn't charge him with stealing or something.

Hell, she probably wouldn't want him back anyway because according to her, he barely earned his keep. She'd do just as well without him and be happier too, not waiting for phone calls from school or wondering when he'd get Maria pregnant. After all, Wade himself was just an accident.

"Here's your A," Mr. B said in English class.

There it was, *The Need To Be Free* test with his name on it, and Mr. B's big red script *A*. He had answered all the short questions correctly, scored one hundred on the multiple choice section, and written an excellent essay.

At the end of class Mr. B called Wade to his desk. "I'm removing the zeros you had for missing assignments. Now if you keep up this kind of work, you'll have an A or B for the quarter." Wade, embarrassed and pleased, mumbled a thank you. "I hear you had some trouble in the office." Wade nodded. "I'm going to put in a word with Mr. Greenberg. Could be we can get those detentions reduced."

"Do you have the absence list for today?"

The sheet did not list Maria, but on a hunch Wade asked to see the principal's list. There it was, Grade 11, Blanchard, Maria. Maybe she'd come in late. His luck was still holding. Who else would have guessed that Maria would be on the principal's list?

He hurried down to the cafeteria to have lunch with her. Actually, she had lunch, and he drank a chocolate milk, which was all he had money for, though he told her he wasn't hungry.

"I suppose you heard about the principal's list," she said. Her hair hid under a kerchief, and she wore no make-up, making her look older.

Wade nodded.

"My father's planting his boots all over everything I try to do." Maria's father had called school and had threatened to call DCYS on her. Between guidance and Mr. Greenberg, she hadn't been to a class yet this morning. She said she wasn't going back to her father's house ever, not even tonight. She'd had it. She'd run away before she'd let anybody make her go back there.

"Did Mr. Greenberg think you'd done something wrong?"

"He was worried I'd move and still try to go to school here. He said the school has a problem with out-of-district students attending Rumford High. He thought I might be afraid of my father and move somewhere out of town."

"You don't look frightened to me." Wade smiled at her. He felt bold with his *A* in his pocket and his girlfriend across the table.

"Mr. Greenberg was apologetic, saying the school would

have to get involved because my social worker would have access to my grades, attendance, any disciplinary report." She bit into her Sloppy Joe, careful to lean over so the juicy sauce fell onto her tray and not her blouse. He thought of her chocolate chin and the napkin in his pocket, more precious than the *A* on the *Need To Be Free* test.

"Sounds like you lose all your privacy."

"I get a juvenile officer who'll probably start me off with a ten o'clock curfew. No late night picnics at the drive-in." She sipped milk from the straw in the carton of milk. He knew she didn't want all those arrangements and restrictions.

"It'd be a lot easier to take off." He spun his chocolate milk in his hands. He hadn't opened it yet. "Be simpler to go to Vermont with me." He reached his hand across the table.

"You're right there." She pulled her tray closer. "I've had enough of my father. Today I'm taking my stuff right out of his place. Tonight I'll go to Lisa's. I could stay with her awhile. After that, I'm not sure."

"You're not afraid of your father?" In an odd way he hoped she'd say yes.

"Steven Blanchard wouldn't dare hurt me physically, but he did threaten to file a CHINS petition on me. Can you believe that? A child in need of supervision? That's him, he's the child. I'll leave the state before I'll let him do that."

He smiled at her, brought his hand back, and opened his milk, praying it wouldn't splash. "I'm thinking of leaving tomorrow."

"Right now I'm so tired I can't think. If you said, here's the car, let's go right now, I might be crazy enough to get in. I wouldn't think about it until we got to Vermont. How far is it to your uncle's?"

"An hour and a half, two."

"I could sleep that long," Maria said, "without a problem."

Wasn't that a sign he should go? A sweet sign, sweeter than the chocolate milk he drained.

Going upstairs to math class, Wade saw John looking glum. "What's the matter, dude?" he asked him.

John hung back outside the door. "Nothing," he said. "Trouble at home."

"Something from last night?"

"No, no, my mother was real happy, thankful for your help. She was worried we were going to have to pay an extra month's rent on the place. She said you put us over the top with your help." The cheer in his words spread no smile on his face.

Still feeling bold, Wade again asked what the trouble was at home.

Instead of answering, John asked Wade if he'd done the math homework. Neither of them had, so they slipped down the stairs and outside to sit on the grassy bank overlooking the parking lot.

"It's my sister," John said. "She didn't even come to school today."

Wade thought of Greenberg's grilling Maria. "How are you going to keep coming to school here if your mother lives in Manchester?"

"We stay with my dad some of the time or my aunt. They both live in Rumford."

"I asked because Maria's going to move out of her house, only we're going to Vermont. You're lucky, dude, your mother didn't make you move. I hope Jen's okay."

John didn't look lucky. "It's hard." John rubbed his cheek with his big hands, especially big hands for a kid barely taller than Wade. "I'm not supposed to say anything. You know last night everybody was so happy and all." Wade waited for him to tell what he was not supposed to tell. John rubbed his knees and let out a big sigh. "Her cat died, Jen's tabby."

For this Jen stayed home, John was depressed and sworn to silence? This was a family tragedy? Right now Wade felt that Maria and he lived in a world far darker than John's. "I like cats and all, but I guess some people take these things very hard. I know when my dog—"

"The thing is she blames herself." John looked at his feet as if he was as mystified as Wade.

"Naturally that makes it worse." In the parking lot Wade saw Riley leave his car and stroll over to the smoking area with that long-legged gait he put on to look studly. Wade wanted to catch him before the period ended because later he might not be able to find Riley.

"See the cat died in the clothes dryer. He crawled in there looking for some place soft and warm, and Jen turned it on. That's why."

Wade held back a surge of snarling laughter, not at Jen or John or even the cat, but at the absurdity of the death, parodying that old joke about sticking the cat in the microwave to dry his fur.

"That's what makes your sister a good person, she takes responsibility. A lesser person would blame someone else."

"It's hard," John said.

"It's not something you just shrug off." Hard though it was, he patted John on the back, then told him he had to talk with Riley.

When Wade asked Riley for a ride to Vermont, skipping the part about already putting enough gas in Riley's tank to drive half way across America, Riley said, "It ain't like I'm a fucking taxi, you know." He stuck his cigarette in his mouth and waved to John. "What's the matter with him, anti-social or something?"

"I can't tell you." As soon as Wade spoke, he knew he'd made a mistake. After being so careful with John, why'd he have to go and make a dumb mistake like that with Riley? Give him a gun, put him in the woods, Wade made no mistakes. Put him in with a bunch of people, his mouth flapped around like an unlatched door in a windstorm.

"You and he break up?"

Wade looked quickly at Riley but saw a too-hard set of the eyebrows and mouth that showed him Riley wasn't even close to serious. Regular Riley held his cigarette underhand, as if waiting for Wade to deliver an answer. "Come on, this is important. I want to take Maria too."

"You ought to get yourself wheels, dude. Hell, you got a girl, you need a car. You work, don't you?"

For a while Wade let Riley rattle on about saving money, making a down payment, buying a car and fixing it yourself, choosing insurance, everything with a dollars and days tag on it, as though Riley had the math of life all figured out. Goddamn motorhead. Wade would never worship cars.

"All I'm asking for is a ride."

"Tell me what John's problem is, I'll think about it."

Wade wanted to ask if Riley had the hots for John, but he'd already made a mistake talking too much. "Sure, that's fair, I tell you, then maybe you'll give us a ride. Some deal that is."

"You don't want to tell me about your boyfriend, don't. You got to do what you got to do." He turned his back to Wade while he sucked down a big drag. "Does Maria know about this relationship?" He laughed until a cough caught him.

Hack up a lung why don't you, Wade thought. He

remembered a bumper sticker he'd seen on a van, GAS, CASH, ASS, OR GRASS, NOBODY RIDES FOR FREE. The way to Riley's heart ran straight through his wallet. "I'll pay you. I'll pay you for your time."

"How much?"

"Ten bucks an hour, over and back. Only you can't tell anybody about it." A sense of secrecy would make Riley feel important.

"When you want to go?"

Wade had already told him, at least once, but again he said, "Tomorrow."

"Ten bucks an hour?"

"Over and back."

"Gas?"

"I filled your tank last week."

"Right. But that was last week, and I been booking all over the place." As the bell rang, Riley snubbed his cigarette. "Oh, what the fuck, I'll be here."

Wade watched John pull himself together to face class. It could be a long time before Wade would see him again. He hadn't seen Ernie in over a year. Thinking about missing people gave Wade a slow, sad taste in his mouth.

A Gift

In the *You And The Law* class Shawn asked the teacher if they'd get to see some guy hang during the courthouse field trip tomorrow. The teacher reminded him it would be a trial, not an execution. "Same difference," said Shawn, "just like school. How about the execution, then the trial?" He noogied Peter and laughed. Wade wondered if Shawn would laugh when he received the punishment he deserved for lighting poor Herman. Wade himself could laugh or stay silent at will.

After class Wade hurried home. He needed money. If he couldn't find any in the house, he could quit and ask Rich for the hold-back, but then Rich might tell his mother. If either Peter or John had a car, they'd give him the ride and not charge him, not even for the gas, but Riley wanted money. And he'd want it up front. No money, no go, that would be Riley's way.

Wade knew a way to make Riley drive them to Vermont without paying him.

He was glad he had kept John's story about his sister's cat a secret. Riley would keep quiet about Wade's plans because it would make him feel like a big deal to break out of his regular mode and contribute to an escape.

Searching through his mother's bureau, Wade saw a

box of condoms. He wondered if his mother had kept the ones he'd stolen from Osco's. Sure enough, an unopened box, same red and white Trojans, lay farther back. He'd have to buy another box if he could get the money. He wouldn't take these now that they'd been in her drawer, but he couldn't risk getting caught swiping a box from Osco's. For Riley he'd need at least forty dollars, or he'd need his gun.

She must have taken all the money in the house. Walking around like the goddamn Bank of Velma with her money and his money and his father's money probably made her feel like she controlled the world. He stuck his hand between mattress and box spring, cautiously as if she might have hidden a spider or a trap in there. No money. Nothing.

In his own room he prepared for lighting out. He would take his gun, backpack, cooking gear, clothes. He'd wear his clothes. He needed his stove, a set of silverware, and a bowl for Maria, if she went with him into the woods. He could stick all that stuff in his backpack. His gun? How could he take his gun to school? He should have told Riley to meet him here. His gun, he could sell his gun. He could easily get fifty bucks for it. It was worth three times that much. He put his camo vest and pants on the bed. Alongside of them he laid his bandoliers and his shotgun, Uncle Andrew's gift. He picked up the gun. He would have to sell it. What other choice did he have?

Eventually he could buy another one. Two incomes at Uncle Andrew's would pay for food and rent with some left over that he could set aside for a gun. He wouldn't ask Maria to work. Of course she might want to so she wouldn't have to rely on him for spending money. He wouldn't put her in the same position as his mother put his father, having to beg for pocket change, even if he did waste it on beer.

A car. Wade had forgotten about a car. With all the roads twisting and winding like mating snakes, Uncle Andrew's trailer probably sat miles from any job. He'd need a car. And insurance.

Someone was outside, on the porch. His mother home early from work? Panicked, he slid the shotgun under his bed, bunched his clothes in the blanket, and ran to her room. Everything looked all right, in its place, nothing to make her suspicious. His heart stuttered like a hard-starting chain saw. She wasn't coming in. Was she waiting on the porch to catch him at something? Maybe she had her arms full and would criticize him for not opening the door as soon as she hit the porch.

He ran to the door. No one stood on the porch or peered in the windows. Two houses down the mail carrier walked the sidewalk. Dipping his hand into the mailbox, Wade pulled out the sole envelope, a thick letter from Uncle Andrew to him, thick with a map? This time his mother would not steal it. It was his alone.

He went straight to his room, put the shotgun back on the bed, and opened the letter. The first thing he saw was the money, tens and twenties, which had thickened the envelope. The letter itself was brief.

Dear Wade,

Figuring you to be down in the dumps and probably more than a little broke, I'm sending you $75 to cheer you up. Can't have my Rumpty-de-Dump nephew unhappy! Now don't worry about the money because it actually came from you. Let's just say your "dear head" figured out a way to send you a cheer-me-up present.

Love,

Uncle Andrew

Wade reread the letter. He counted the money, two twenties, three tens, and a five. Uncle Andrew was thinking of him, that he knew for sure. Still, he didn't feel better, though now he had the money to pay Riley without having to sell his shotgun. Where had Uncle Andrew found seventy-five extra dollars? He couldn't even afford a telephone. Again he read the letter.

"Dear head" why had Uncle Andrew—deer head. Deer head, Wade's buck. Uncle Andrew had sold it for seventy-five dollars. Oh, God! His achievement, his gift to Uncle Andrew, gone, sold. Things had turned so bad that he'd sold Wade's buck and sent the money to cheer Wade up. Wade hoped Uncle Andrew had kept some money for himself, but he didn't know how much a stuffed head was worth. Wade had to go to Vermont. Whatever doubts

had held him back disappeared with the deer head. Wade would help Uncle Andrew financially, cheer him up, and he'd buy the buck back. The trophy would be on the trailer wall as soon as Wade could put it there.

By the time Wade reached work, he'd bought condoms, a new bowl, a silverware set, and even two boxes of shells at the Hawkeye Store, since they were there, he was there, and he had the money. With enough left over to pay Riley and even buy some food, he was ready. He'd planned, counted accurately, and he was prepared. Uncle Andrew would approve. Wade didn't worry about his mother taking his money because she'd have no way of knowing he had any. Nor would she suspect he carried anything in his backpack other than school junk. He'd even remembered to bring his *Need To Be Free* test with the trophy *A* to show to Rich.

Rich congratulated him with a handshake and a squeeze on the back of his neck. "Look at this," he said. "A perfect score. I could never get a perfect score in English." He said nothing about Wade's lying to him the other night. Had Wade's mother really told Rich that Wade had lied?

Everything seemed good except Maria wasn't there. She'd phoned in to say she needed the day off for a family emergency. Rich refused to say any more because it was confidential.

Dishes from the dining room piled in the trays, leaving him little time to think. His hands, tough though they were from heat and alkali soap (like soaking them in a desert,

Rich had told him), had regained their sensitivity. Every rack he pulled from the Hobart spattered scalding drops on the backs of his hands, each glass he set on the tray seared his fingertips, steel fibers bore into the cracks in his palms and finger joints as he scrubbed the burned pots.

He hoped he could get a better job than this in Vermont. Being able to put in a regular day shift would help him land something other than restaurant work, though he didn't know what it would be.

Rich always told him, "Learn to cook and stay away from the sauce, that's the ticket. A good chef in one of these fancy resorts will make more than the owner if he can stay away from the sauce."

Rich didn't understand that Wade already knew how to take care of himself in the woods or at home. As for money, he needed only enough to pay the bills and buy back his buck's head. He didn't tell Rich any of this, not only because he wanted to keep his move to Uncle Andrew's a secret, but also because he didn't want to hurt Rich's feelings by rejecting his advice. He would be hurting Rich tomorrow by not showing up for work and, worse, by taking one of the waitresses with him.

He wished work were over so he could plan with Maria exactly where to meet and when. He wanted to tell her not to be embarrassed when she saw him carrying a big garbage bag because that would hold his shotgun, which he'd almost had to sell. He'd tell her about the buck's head.

Above him hung a gummed strip of fly paper coated with the dead black insects. He'd have to replace that and empty the dump barrels, and—a parade of dirty jobs marched in front of him, blocking his way to see Maria.

Grabbing a stack of dinner plates, he rounded the corner of his area, the hot porcelain burning his hands. His mother burst in from the dining room bearing an overloaded tray. The wet floor forced him to walk slowly. Heat from the plates stabbed through flesh to reach his bones. She stood in his way. Burn, bad burning, soaked from the smooth dishes through his body, his bones becoming searing china. He dropped them, the entire stack. They exploded like a gunshot.

"Jesus Christ!" he shouted at his mother.

"I didn't touch him," she told Rich.

"What's the matter with you?" Rich handed a broom and dustpan to Wade, who was already picking up the pieces of china. "Don't yell at your mother."

Wade said nothing. His fingers felt like paws, awkwardly shuffling the mess around, dropping more pieces, cutting his flesh on jagged edges. He filled his palms, walked to the dump barrel, and went back for more. Rich wheeled the barrel over to Wade's mess. He must have held back a hundred criticisms, including asking Wade why he wasn't smart enough to move the barrel to the job. His not saying anything made Wade feel more stupid, more guilty, more frustrated with the sense that Rich was right.

After work he took a cab to Maria's. What the hell, he still had more than enough money to pay Riley. This was an emergency. Now that his hands had cooled off, his face felt aflame. He hoped Maria would answer the door, but if she didn't, that was okay. He could deal with her father. Hadn't she said her father wouldn't hurt her, he was afraid to hurt her? Steven Blanchard, a man afraid of a girl, was not about to scare Wade.

Maria's stepmother in tee-shirt and jeans answered his knock. Out of breath from running up the stairs, Wade held Maria's name in his mouth a moment. With a wave of her hand the woman, looking fearfully down the hall, tried to shoo Wade away. Though his face burned and his heart thumped, he wouldn't put up with this.

"Maria," he said. "I want to see Maria."

"You'll see the cops, that's who you'll see!"

Pushing past his wife, Steven Blanchard in white trousers and a stained, unbuttoned white cook's shirt blocked the doorway. Wade remembered he worked in the kitchen at the private school out past the hospital.

"I ain't done anything." A startling pang of guilt jabbed his gut. How did Maria's father know? "I just want to talk to her."

"She ain't here."

On top of everything else, Steven Blanchard was a liar. Well, why wouldn't he be? According to Maria he was a criminal. Wouldn't a criminal lie? Wade hoped the raised voices would bring Maria to the doorway, especially since she'd said her father didn't scare her.

"Where is she?" He was going to say, don't tell me she's at work, but he waited to hear Steven Blanchard lie about that.

"I'll let the cops find her. Now get out of here."

"I'll have a look first."

Wade raised his arm to brush past Maria's father. Before he could step inside the apartment, his arm twisted behind his back, his body reversed, and his throat closed, choked by the forearm across it.

"You little fuck!" Steven Blanchard yelled. Wade's back and arm hurt. His feet tripped together. "I told you she ain't here!"

Wade's nose clogged and made him howl as he smashed into the wall. He turned and ran at Steven Blanchard. A quick punch low in his belly doubled him over. As the door shut and locked behind him, he retched a little sour liquid. Holding his stomach and breathing through his mouth, he went down the stairs. Try as he might, he could not remember the name of the friend Maria had said she would stay the night with.

The Hunt

When he woke up the next morning, Wade's stomach hurt. He told his mother he wouldn't be going to Big Rich's this afternoon.

"If you're well enough to go to school, you're well enough to go to work," she said.

"I'm not sure I'm going to school either."

"You'd better go to school," his father said. "They call us when you don't."

"If you don't go to work, you call Rich and explain," his mother said, "because I'm not going to tell him. I'm sick of your lies."

She could only understand his truth as lies. Maybe it wasn't her fault.

After they left he stayed in bed, his stomach still hurting, his mind wandering circles in a confusing thicket. *Neuromancer*, the new sci-fi novel his friend Peter had given him, couldn't keep his attention because he wasn't in the mood for a lot of computer fantasy. Fantasy no longer interested him. His mother's accusations sucked his energy as if he were trudging through swampy ground, muck pulling every boot step into the black earth. He knew he couldn't lie in bed like some baby.

Wade wanted to vomit. Right now, like a baby spitting

up his food, he would toss his insides. Sitting opposite his mother's chair, he gripped the edges of the table. He could puke right across the table, spray his guts out. The sides of the table bore the grime and gunk that had encrusted the table when Velma had brought it home.

"It's free," she'd said, "so don't complain. Clean it."

After hot water and rubbing hadn't worked, he'd used a knife and accidentally cut a chip out of the surface. Then she'd sworn at him, telling him to leave it alone before he dug it into a mess.

He took one of his father's beers out of the fridge and gurgled down a big swallow before the yeasty, sour-bread taste overwhelmed him. Setting the beer on the table, he held his stomach, full of pain and nausea. Another swig and he quit.

He went to his room, where everything was clean and neat, only the lingering smells of smoke and fat reminding him he lived in the same apartment with his mother. He had no suitcase because he owned only what he used. Should he jam all his stuff in paper bags? One thing for certain, once he left, he wasn't coming back. He wouldn't even stack things on the porch so that Riley could drive him over to pick them up. No, this was it, the end, a clean break, out the door and down the road, off to do good in the world as a man should. Rescue Maria and help Uncle Andrew who told him, "Let your light so shine before men that they may see your good works."

How could he do good if he had always to fight against doing bad? If he stayed here, he would do wrong, the temptation was too great.

In a couple of minutes his shotgun lay on his bed, along with two bandoliers, a box of shells, his camo clothes, a canteen, silverware, bowls, two metal dishes, and his backpack. By the wall three cardboard beer boxes he'd scrounged from his father held his clothes: underwear, socks, two pairs of pants, two shirts, three tee-shirts. He left a note on them. *Give these to the poor.*

He dressed in his camo, folding his shirt and cord jeans and stacking them on one of the clothes boxes. Then he started filling the bandoliers with shells.

Okay, he told himself, you're getting smart. You're going to get out, and you're going to help Maria get out too. You're skinny and short, but you're not helpless, not a helpless little kid, not a baby. He stuffed his shotgun into a garbage bag, grabbed a bottle of wine his mother had in the refrigerator, and set off for the high school.

He felt better with his shotgun in his hand and his filled bandoliers across his chest. Maria had never seen him with his gun and ammo and his camo jacket which made him look a little heavier. She'd see he could take charge of things and cut through the bullshit. Already his stomach felt better.

Wade couldn't find Riley's car in the student parking lot.

Twice Wade walked through all the rows, even checking out the faculty area and the street across from the store, only to discover that he'd missed Maria too. Now she'd be in class, and he'd have to get her out. Riley must have come in too late to find a space in the lot. Probably his gray primer beater sat down at the athletic field or over at the state hospital. He'd been conceited enough to go to class and make Wade find him instead of just sitting in his car by the entrance. Riley was like that, always making Wade come to him like some servant, pump the gas into his car. Good thing Riley wore sneakers, or he'd've wanted his shoes shined too.

Carrying his gun, Wade wasn't going to be mistaken for anybody's servant. Maybe he wouldn't even pay Riley for the ride. After all he'd given Riley plenty of gas. No, he'd pay Riley because he'd made a deal, even if it was a bad one, and what's right is right. He didn't want to arrive at Uncle Andrew's lame with a broken promise.

He did want to get there by noon, though. Besides Maria's chocolate stained napkin wrapped in plastic, he carried Uncle Andrew's letter but no map. The letter's return address would guide him to the Vermont trailer where his uncle needed his help, no matter how much his mother denied it. With his gun for hunting, some Reese's Peanut Butter Cups for energy, and the bottle of wine to celebrate, Wade was ready to be on the road.

After they got to Brattleboro, they'd have to ask

directions. How long would that take? He wouldn't put up with Riley saying anything about having to head back to his job before they reached Uncle Andrew's. It was Riley's fault they weren't on the road right now. Riley wouldn't pull any bullshit on him.

At eight o'clock, five minutes after he should have been sitting in class, Wade walked up the concrete squares to the side door of Rumford High School. For a moment the new risen sun caught the breeze swirling in Wade's long hair and cast angelic highlights in its frizzled ends. By the long first step stood a white cylinder with a blue top, into which for the past two years Wade had dropped his VeryFine Juice bottles. Not wanting to walk through the hallways of Rumford High School carrying a garbage bag, Wade pulled out his shotgun, balled up the green plastic, and tossed it at the dump can. He missed. What the hell, he'd shove it into the can when he came back out of the school.

Inside the door he patted the bottle of wine in his jacket and then stared up the staircase that rose with landings between each of the three floors. No one looked down on him. Isolated, he stood in this four story chute as if it could lead him to heaven or to hell. Half a flight up, he walked into the first floor hallway. Outside the main office he stopped and stared the length of the corridor, quiet and lonely, leading to other empty corridors, a dark tunnel he hoped never to see again.

He could walk right in the office and ask Mr. Greenberg

for Riley's schedule. Or like the good Indian he could scout out Riley's first period class. Pain jolted his stomach. He leaned against a locker as he might lean against a friendly tree if he stumbled in the woods. He could ask Mr. Greenberg for Riley's schedule, or he could cruise the hallways like hunter's paths, old logging roads, Indian trails, all the ways he knew so well in the woods.

In the woods you had to be prepared, ready, alert, but no one nagged and criticized you until you were so mixed up you lost yourself standing on your own feet right in your own room. Learning on his own and from his uncle, he had never joined Scouts or Outing Club, who wanted to teach you what you had to see in the woods as if you couldn't see for yourself. It had gotten so Wade didn't look in mirrors for fear he wouldn't recognize the reflection.

Still, he recognized he had duties. No one else in the family would help Uncle Andrew. Maria would help, of course, though he knew he had to rescue her so she could finish high school and enjoy her life the way she had a right to. That was how he would light up the world.

Last week Mr. Greenberg told Wade not to quit school, talking to him with school wisdom, as if school wisdom was like woods wisdom, but Mr. Greenberg didn't understood about lighting the world. School taught you to play games where you beat people in order to prepare you for life. Wade didn't have time to explain it to Mr. Greenberg.

He couldn't explain it to his mother because Velma Rule

believed the world was a dark place. She didn't want him to help Uncle Andrew at all. Wade was tired of explaining. Maria understood. And Riley didn't have to understand. All Riley had to do was give them a ride to Vermont.

Wade's stomach stopped crying. He set off to find Riley. Not that he was worried about finding Riley. He wasn't worried about anything. In fact he felt good, ready to free himself, rescue Maria, and aid his crippled Uncle Andrew. In a school of twelve hundred students, not counting the few who were cutting today, he was sure he could find two. He knew the place as well as he knew the patch of fields and woods he'd hunted back in Newfound or the plot of one of the fat books he was always reading.

Shotgun at the end of his arm, Wade walked beyond the corridor that formed the science wing, including Ms. Plizak's room. A little dizziness reminded him of the beer he'd swigged at home, though he could still think straight. The beer took the edge off his jittery stomach, his jelly bones. As he concentrated, the sway in his body disappeared. Walking smoothly, he passed the open door to the guidance department. No one called out to him. Pushing through the doors at the end of the first floor, he stopped in the stairway landing to decide between going up or down. Up led to two floors of classrooms, English, math, social studies, foreign languages, down led to drafting and science. Up where there were more rooms was his best bet for finding Riley, up carried the odds.

Half a flight up he arrived at a landing with long windows. Along the painted brick walls were posters, always posters, the billboards of the school, he called them. Do this, do that, join us, be us. Earlier in the school year it was VOTE FOR ME, then COME TO THE DANCE (Be There Or Be Square), and now, IF YOU HAVE A PROBLEM WITH DRUGS OR ALCOHOL OR IF YOU KNOW SOMEONE WHO DOES... Wade didn't read the rest of it. He put the muzzle of his shotgun to the poster. He could blow it right off the wall. He broke open the shotgun and slid two shells into the barrels. Foolish walls sang the siren songs of groups and cliques and teams, calling him, whom they couldn't understand, to join them and become one of them. Bodysnatchers.

Through the long windows he could see the sun shining down on the parking lot. He'd rather be walking in the woods right now, with or without the shotgun, but he couldn't walk all the way to Vermont before his mother called the cops. Nor could he hitchhike with a gun, which left him with the job of finding Riley.

Right now he could climb out onto the roof, stand there, and start firing into the air. He had enough shells in his bandolier to make everyone come running. He'd like to shoot out windshields of the cars that filled the parking lot and spray flying glass to catch the sunlight, like Fourth of July in the daytime. He switched the shotgun's safety off and then on again.

Up two flights of stairs, down the third floor corridor, Wade hunted, peering into classrooms. Back to the second floor he looked into the fishbowl where Maria took English, but he couldn't see her. There was only one way to find out where Riley was. Although it was bold, he wasn't coming back here anyway, so what difference did it make? If they got pissy about it, he'd claim it was a family emergency. It was, wasn't it?

In the principal's office Mr. Greenberg was dealing with Charley Lovejoy, accused (and guilty) of eating a loaf of bread, an institutional size bottle of catsup, half a dozen hot dogs, and several packages of Twinkies from the cafeteria last night. Charley wouldn't be punished because Charley suffered from Prader-Willi Syndrome. Legally Charley was a nineteen year old adult, scholastically a senior, mentally and physically a child, maybe nine or ten, barred forever by Prader-Willi from entering adolescence.

At seven this morning the cook had reported the theft. "There must have been a herd of them in here last night," she'd said. "Animals."

Mr. Greenberg hated when people spoke of kids that way. Besides, it was only one kid, Charley Lovejoy, whom Prader-Willi had made an appetite with legs, a boy with no full in his tank. Mr. Greenberg thought Charley was lucky his family could pay for the stolen food.

"You'll have to stay out of the cafeteria, Charley," Mr.

Greenberg said. The answer probably lay in better security. The night custodians didn't always lock the door to the cafeteria kitchen. At home Charley's parents had installed locks on all the kitchen cabinets and the refrigerator.

As Mr. Greenberg patted Charley's shoulder, Wade Rule stepped into the office doorway. He was holding a shotgun. A bandolier of shells decorated his camo-covered chest. Mr. Greenberg thought he must be presenting a demonstration for a class, show-and-tell about hunting. He was glad Wade was still in school.

"I assume you want to leave that with me," Mr. Greenberg said.

"No!" Then, without saying anything else, Wade slowly raised the barrel until it pointed at Mr. Greenberg. "No one takes my gun."

Mr. Greenberg felt a huge, dry doughnut form in his throat. "In that case I'll have to call the police," he said and with his fingertips pushed the door closed. Immediately he buzzed his secretary and told her to call the police. "Tell them we have a student in the building with a gun."

"What's going on, Mr. Greenberg?" Charley asked. "Is he going to hurt somebody?"

Mr. Greenberg rushed out from his office. Wade was gone.

At seven-thirty that morning Maria Blanchard left her friend Lisa's house to walk to the court-appointed lawyer's

Centre Street office. Lisa wished her luck, but Maria said she didn't need luck. She needed to be practical if she were going to get out of the rat's nest that her father called home. The lawyer, too, was practical, insisting that she come early to miss as little school as possible. She approved of practicality. She wished she could give some of hers to poor Wade Rule. God knew he needed it, what with his fantasies of running away with her to Vermont. Even taking himself there seemed a fantasy.

The lawyer, a short, cheerful man, kept his fair hair cropped but not spiked. His suit, a soft blue wool that must have come from Boston, closely fit his trim body. He wore his confidence well. Maria's will weakened because she feared he would ask about her mother. If he did, she would have to drag her confidence up by the hair and say her mother had swallowed lye, right in the kitchen, seven years ago. She'd want the lawyer to know her mother's suicide wasn't the reason she'd come.

"I want myself declared a ward of the state."

"Your father wants you to stay with him." The lawyer leaned forward, his elbows sliding gracefully on the polished desk.

"He filed a CHINS petition on me," Maria said. "I know what a CHINS petition is."

"He said you ran away." A paper between the lawyer's hands prompted his questions. His eyes softly stared, watching how she answered.

"He knew where I was." Not only had she told her father where she was going, she'd left her friend's telephone number.

"Why do you want to leave home?"

"Crazy bitch, stubborn cunt," Maria said. "These are his pet names for me." Often when she studied, he'd burst into the room, half-drunk, sweep her homework to the floor and thrash her book in her face.

"When did the abuse start, after your mother died?"

"No, not when Mother died." Three years ago, when she'd started high school, everything had started. Not just the swearing, yelling, insulting, until words bore the bitter-sour smell of beer and garlic, but also the snowy stare as if he were looking at a bill he didn't intend to pay. He would leave in the morning for work with not so much as a grunt.

She told the lawyer she knew why her father berated her. She'd criticized him, his lazy, shiftless, purposeless life. He saw no value in anything and sneered at anyone who did. "'Look, you uppity cunt,' he said, 'stick those schoolbooks up your ass, you wouldn't have so much to say.'"

"Did he ever physically abuse you?"

"No," she said. "I think he's afraid. He's a coward."

"Are you positive he doesn't care about you?" Gracefully, the lawyer slid his arms back across the desk. "People show love in different ways, different people—different ways, even weird ways, sometimes—"

"I'm sixteen and a half," Maria said. "I know the difference between love and hate."

"You'd better be sure," the lawyer said, "because you'll find the state a cold parent. Even though you've done nothing wrong, you'll live under the rules and regs of the court. You won't even be able to leave New Hampshire without the court's permission."

Poor Wade. He'd be so unhappy when she'd tell him she couldn't go to Vermont with him to visit his uncle, but at least she'd have a reason he could accept. He was such a needy boy, she wished she could help him more. Of course she didn't want to lead him into thinking she wanted to be more than friends. Maybe he'd actually go to Vermont this weekend, and his uncle would help him sort things out. Wade's always wanting to help someone was so much like his mother, only he couldn't see it. The one time Maria had tried to point it out to him, he'd rejected it as if she'd offered him spider soup. Velma Rule had helped her at the restaurant, as had Rich, always allowing her time off when she needed to make all these arrangements.

By the time she walked back to school first period would be over, and she could find Wade. She'd tell him about the lawyer. She wouldn't tell Wade how he was like his mother. He had a sweet side, which she'd never seen in his mother, a side that liked the woods and simple things. Some people might call him childlike, but she knew it for sweetness. When she saw Wade, she'd tell him how sweet he was because she was sure he needed to hear that.

Wade hurried down the corridor. He had to find Riley and
Maria before the cops arrived. Cops. Wade did not want to
deal with cops like Slim Jim, swearing at him, scaring him,
never thinking for one minute that Wade might be right in
his thinking and actions. Probably he should have hidden
the shotgun outside somewhere until he found Riley or
left it in the garbage bag. But there was no absolutely safe
place to hide the gun, no place he could be certain would
protect it from thieves. Nor did he want to walk around
with a damn garbage bag under his arm like pathetic old
Herman who dug through the dump barrels collecting
aluminum cans. What name would they call him then?
Herman's boy? Son of Herman?

Why did Mr. Greenberg have to call the cops? All
Wade wanted was Riley's class, the room number. He
didn't need a personal escort. He could find it on his own.
Mr. Greenberg, without even hearing what he wanted,
said, *I assume you're going to leave that with me*. He didn't wait
for Wade to explain, like nothing Wade had to say could
be so important that it couldn't be interrupted. And why
would Mr. Greenberg think Wade would want to leave his
shotgun there? It was one of the few things he was taking
with him from Rumford. He'd bet Mr. Greenberg had
never hunted in his life.

Wade should have just said, Where's Riley? We're

going on a field trip. Or any old lie. He could have said something. The field trip would have worked because there was a field trip today. The next time someone asked him something, he'd just say Riley was giving him and Maria a ride to the courthouse for a field trip, and that'd be that. They wouldn't ask to take his gun.

When he'd pointed the gun at Mr. Greenberg, Mr. Greenberg didn't give him any bullshit. That was the point, wasn't it? No more bullshit. He pointed the gun and a light went on. No more bullshit.

That was what he'd tell Maria. No more bullshit. He'd have to tell Maria in such a way that she wouldn't think he was bragging. He'd tell Maria, I came here for you. I walked around the high school looking for Riley, could've been hours, could've been New York City, could've been the moon. I walked all over the surface of the moon looking for goddamn Riley to give us a ride to Vermont. Mr. Greenberg about shit his pants when I strolled into his office with my shotgun looking for Riley. Mr. Greenberg got the shakes so bad he couldn't punch the buttons on his phone to call the cops. Just looking at me and this gun brought him right to a standstill. He saw the light. And, for once, no bullshit. No more bullshit.

That was bragging. It was all bragging. Wade found it easier to brag than to say, Sickness came all over me, my stomach especially, until I thought of seeing you. Then I felt better, and I knew I'd feel all better if I could see you, be with you, hold you.

Who could doubt him? Mr. Greenberg knew he was serious, knew he was not here for bullshit. All the way to Vermont he'd say, I love you. He'd climb a tree and shout it to her, as soon as they crossed the river into Vermont. But first he had to go through all this bullshit. Why did he have to endure all this bullshit? He wouldn't bullshit himself any longer. He knew that for certain.

He had to find Riley to give him a ride. Wade climbed the stairway again, muttering half aloud, "Where the fuck is he? Where the fuck is he?"

Having first period supervisory duty allowed Mr. B to photocopy just before class. Standing in the second floor department office, he aligned the sixty-five copies of his *In Cold Blood* study guide. Then he patrolled the upper two halls. The second floor usually remained quiet, but he thought about checking the boys' room. Just a week ago Mr. B had found a kid passed out in a locked stall. Mr. Greenberg had cc'd Mr. B on the letter to the boy's father.

Dear Mr. LaSeur:

On Thursday morning your son Ralph was drunk in the second floor boys' room. Nearly dead drunk. Only the aid of a caring teacher prevented a serious tragedy. A teacher, I might add, with no responsibility for toilet duty. A teacher suffering from back problems, who unselfishly scaled a wall to help the unconscious Ralph.

Ralph had begun to aspirate his own vomit. As close as we can determine he had consumed the better part of a bottle of vodka. The teacher, after removing Ralph's face from his vomit, called the school nurse. The school nurse called the rescue squad. They took Ralph to the emergency room.

For his sake, for yours, get Ralph some help. His guidance counselor will advise you on available programs. Until Ralph has enrolled in a program, he will not be permitted to re-enter the school.

Today the bathroom was empty, but from outside in the hallway, Mr. B heard muffled swearing. When he opened the door, all was silent.

Wade hoped Mr. B hadn't seen him. There was no point in talking to Mr. B now because he knew Mr. B didn't have Riley in class this period. Wade hurried down to the caf because Riley might be squandering time sitting there or outside with a coffee and a cigarette.

From the caf foyer Wade scoped out the long tables. No Riley. He saw no one he knew who owned a car. If you had a car and no first period, why would you drive to school at this hour? Just to sit in the caf?

Outside in the smoking area the empty benches sat lonely in the cold sunlight. He had forgotten that the smoking area was closed this period, so naturally Riley wouldn't be here. Not that "closed" made any difference to Wade because he and his gun could go wherever he wanted. No bullshit. Was someone about to give him detentions for being in an out-of-bounds area now that he'd stepped out of the bounds of school and Mother and all the crap they thought made up life? He was skipping their life and taking no penalties for it. No one was here to give him anything, neither detentions, nor a ride.

Where was Riley? Maybe Wade should stroll out on the street to flag down a passing car like kids in horror movies after their cars break down and the monster's killed some old guard or their mother or something. Their mother! What bullshit!

"Where the fuck is Riley?" Wade mumbled when he was back in the empty hallway. He knew where Riley would be second period because then Riley'd be in *Advanced Reading*, the class right on the first floor, but Wade would not wait until second period. He'd waited long enough. Wade strode down the hall, his hand wrapped around the trigger guard. He didn't have to look dark and mean, not carrying a shotgun. The shotgun had its own dark look. Riley.

Six miles from the high school Riley stretched until his toes trapped themselves in the tight sheet at the foot of the bed. He was chill, really chill. Once a quarter he took a day off from school, and today was the day. In his father's apartment only the clicks and snaps of expanding heat fins broke the silence.

His father, knowing Riley was going to take the day off,

had gotten up, eaten, and turned up the heat, all without saying a word. Riley appreciated the quiet. He was not a morning person.

After his shower, Riley let his hair air dry while he slathered peanut butter on toast, his favorite breakfast. Later he was going to take Peter to look at VCRs at the mall. Peter, the video nut, already owned two VCRs. Peter never got enough of videos, like Wade with those goddamn horror books. Riley didn't mind carting these guys around, as long as they paid for the gas. Pretty soon he'd spin past the school and have a laugh at all those poor bastards locked up in school.

Shit, he was supposed to take to Wade to Vermont today. And get paid for it. Grabbing his breakfast in one hand, his keys in the other, he hurried out of the apartment. Through the chewy-crunchy peanut butter toast, Riley mumbled his wordless song.

Stages

Wade felt the day slipping away from him, deer wandering off to bed down somewhere he'd never see them, way beyond even rifle range and he only had a shotgun. He had to find someone. On the basement floor Wade saw John in drafting class, but he was talking to the teacher. Before Wade could get John's attention, he heard someone running, so he ran to the first floor. Now, down the science wing he headed for Ms. Plizak's room. She would help him without any bullshit. She wouldn't say STAY IN SCHOOL, STAY WITH YOUR PARENTS, SEE A COUNSELOR. There it was, the good old bio room with the glass in the door covered with drawings of water life. To avoid interruptions to her class, Ms. Plizak always covered the glass with student work. "Anytime the door is open," she'd told Wade, "come right in. I'm always glad to see you."

Not only wasn't the door open, he couldn't see inside to tell if she had a class. She'd hate it if he burst in on a class. Nice as she was, she hated anything that interfered with her teaching.

Maria should be in her English class in the second floor fishbowl, though he hadn't been able to see her when he'd passed by before. Maybe he hadn't looked hard enough, distracted by looking for Riley at the same time. This time he'd find her.

In the second floor English Department office, Mr. B again heard mumbled cursing in the hallway. He looked out into the empty hallway. Near the end, from the fishbowl, the teacher stepped out and beckoned to him.

"One of the students said a boy walked by here carrying a gun," she said. "He was staring into our classroom. She said he headed upstairs."

Mr. B suspected she was goofing on him, something he himself was known for. "Maybe it was a ray gun," he said. "Was he all green?"

"The girl said he seemed to be looking for someone."

"Probably a custodian with a broom," he told her. "I'll see what I can find." He started up the stairs to the third floor.

In his third floor social studies class Peter smudged his notes when Shawn Burns pushed back in his chair. He whispered to Peter, "Tell Mac we got to get out early for the fucking field trip." The field trip to watch a trial was scheduled to leave the beginning of second period. "Maybe we'll see the bastard get the death penalty."

"They don't give the death penalty for negligent homicide," Peter said. "I'm not going to lie to Mac. You tell him yourself."

Shawn rolled his eyes and raised his eyebrows. On his

smooth, round face they looked like bruises. "Don't be a pussy."

Peter looked over Shawn's head, but a minute later he raised his hand.

Shawn smirked at Peter as they packed themselves out the classroom's back door and down the stairway. "I knew you could do it," Shawn said. "Mac's got the hots for your skinny little ass."

"Can't you ever just enjoy a favor?" Peter said. Sometimes he wished he wouldn't do favors for guys who never did favors for him.

On the first floor near the office they ran into Wade Rule in a camo jacket crossed with bandoliers and carrying a shotgun.

"You can't go on the court field trip with a gun," Peter said to Wade. "Were you doing a hunting—"

"He's entering the Rambo look-alike contest," Shawn said.

"You seen Riley?" Wade said.

Wade hadn't found anyone except John. Now here were Peter and Shawn Burns, neither of whom could give him a ride. Maria wasn't in class. Even if he did find Riley, he'd have to ride out to The Mills and make Maria's stepmother tell him where Maria was. The stepmother, retarded or crazy, never acted mean, so she'd probably tell him. But he had to find Riley first. He had to find somebody who could get him to Uncle Andrew's.

Velma Rule took a breather before the eight-twenty rush arrived. On her way to the kitchen Rich asked her if Wade were all right.

"I'm just going to call him now," she said. Back in the little office, she lit a cigarette and wondered what she should say to Wade. One day last week Maria had told Velma she was worried about Wade.

"He bothering you?"

"He talks about you a lot, real angry sometimes."

"He's rebelling," Velma had said. "It's just a stage. You're a teenager. You know about stages."

Velma called her house. The long rings floated in the receiver like distant sirens. Where could the boy be? She called the high school, but oddly no one answered. She told Rich she was going to take an hour and go up to the high school. "There is school today, isn't there?"

If Wade and Maria were in Riley's car right now, heading for Vermont, they could eat lunch with Uncle Andrew. Instead he was standing in the corridor with Peter and Shawn. He'd like to hear Shawn shut up. He'd like more light too. It was dark as a damn tomb in this school hallway. That's what his mother would say to him when he'd sit in his bedroom with a book. "How can you read in here?" she'd ask. "It's dark as a tomb." She knew about such things. She was deadly.

Running up the three short stairs from the cafeteria to the basement floor, Mr. Greenberg saw no one in the hall. At the first floor landing he stepped into the corridor. He realized that he had started to move cautiously. He had always ridiculed the false dichotomy between school and the "real world." Now Wade had superseded all realities with his shotgun.

All the way down the corridor, across from the main office door, stood Wade and two boys. Mr. Greenberg couldn't identify the boys from here, two-thirds the length of a football field away, but he could tell Wade Rule by the shotgun. Halfway to the three boys, Mr. Greenberg crossed the hall and entered the main office complex by the guidance door.

Peter, still wondering about Wade's outfit, asked him what he was doing.

"Riley. I need a ride," Wade said. "I'm taking Maria to Uncle Andrew's." He moved a wine bottle into the same hand that held the shotgun and with the other hand fished from his pocket a chocolate stained napkin. "Oh, shit. This is the old dark place where she used to live, an out-of-place map."

"Where do you want to go?" Peter asked, hoping to calm Wade. He had never seen Wade so screwed up. Wade wasn't drunk either, though he smelled of booze and was hard to understand. He was always hard to understand.

"Vermont. My uncle's trailer. Want a drink?" Wade held out the bottle to Peter and Shawn. When they both shook their heads, he tipped it to his lips.

Peter noticed only a little wine slid into Wade's mouth in slow, pink bubbles. It was a show-off trick, something he never expected from Wade, something Shawn would do. Peter knew Wade was showing off, but he was dangerously close to real trouble. Peter hated trouble.

"What's the name of the town?" Peter asked. How the hell Wade would find his uncle, Peter couldn't imagine. Nor could he imagine what Wade was looking at now, his head swinging back and forth like a crazy robot. The doors to the east stairs were closed. Peter glanced through the glass panels at the landing, expecting to see their social studies teacher preparing to take them to the courthouse. Instead, it looked like the court had come to the school, at least the entire police force. The west stairs had no doors, but it, too, was crowded with cops all the way to the outside doors.

"You're my hostages," Wade told Peter and Shawn.

Lighting
the World

In the main office with microphone in hand, Mr. Greenberg faced the p.a. system's array of flip switches and plastic buttons and pressed the All Call switch on the metal console. He told everyone to stay in their classrooms. "Close your doors and stay in your classrooms," he repeated. "Do not send anyone to the office." He knew that his every word shouted from the speaker over Wade Rule's head as well as from the classroom speakers. With a quick thumb push, he shut off the microphone.

"Where should we go?" the English secretary asked. Three other office workers joined her and without waiting for Mr. Greenberg's decision, crowded into the narrow corridor away from the main door. "Shut off the bell," the secretary said, "so it won't release the students." As Mr. Greenberg turned off the automatic bell system, the telephone rang. No one answered it.

In his basement floor classroom John heard his name being shouted. He opened the classroom door and saw more cops than he'd seen in his whole life, a couple of them way down the hall shouting his name.

"Get back inside," a cop ordered him.

"But I'm John."

"Not you, a kid upstairs with a gun." The cop walked toward John. "We don't want anyone hurt."

"But I'm John Adams."

"Then who's that boy up there with the gun?"

"I don't know," John said. "Is someone after me?"

Halfway down the first floor corridor Mr. Greenberg heard the cops yelling. "Adams! John!" The name echoed crazily off the walls. The police must have mistaken Wade for John. Jesus Christ, Mr. Greenberg thought, they couldn't even get his name right. Back to the end of the science wing, down the stairs and through the doors to the basement floor, he found a blue army. The first cop he saw he told, "The boy's name is Wade, Wade Rule." Then he hurried back upstairs. No state troopers or SWAT team, all Rumford cops. Now they shouted, "Wade! Wade! Rule! Wade! Rule!"

Alone in the second floor hallway, Mr. B walked the corridor, checking that all the classroom doors were closed. At the hall's end he pushed open the door to the landing and stepped halfway to the rail where he heard shouts rising up the stairwell. "Wade! Rule! Wade!" Gradually, he peered over the railing. A flight and a half below, between the basement and the first floor, stood Sergeant Gallagher with a shotgun. Mr. B could see another Rumford cop lying on the stairs. Had Wade been the boy with the gun who had walked past the fishbowl classroom? Back in the corridor, he took out his master key and locked every classroom door on the floor.

The shouting below continued, "Wade! Wade! Rule! Rule!"

Wade Rule?

Mr. B, head slightly over the railing, listened to the cops calling, "Wade! Wade! Wade! Rule! Rule!" Irritating, harshly echoing, the name became a command, a sharp bounce of sound that slammed into Mr. B's ears. Alone in this long, hollow, blue corridor, he hovered at the edge of pounding noise.

Wade Rule?

He'd always liked Wade. Maybe the boy would listen to him. He started very slowly down the stairs.

On the first floor, Peter watched Wade tip the bottle of pink wine back to his lips. Again most of the wine stayed in the bottle, Wade fake-chugging it. Peter deliberately ignored the police so as not to get Wade p.o.'d. Wade seemed crazy but not angry, not yet.

"Don't you want a drink?" Wade asked, pointing the bottle mouth at Shawn. "Be my friend?" A chill shook Peter's back, as if it were the gun, not the bottle, Wade pointed.

"Not me, me, man," Shawn stammered.

Peter, too, refused.

Wade threw the bottle against the wall and watched the wine run down to stain the carpet. Now he had both hands free for the gun.

"Want me to fire it?" he asked. "Want to see me shoot it?" The excitement in his voice mixed with menace, though neither showed on his face.

Shawn and Peter shook their heads. Shells lined Wade's chest, shot after shot, shot after shot. There were two in the gun already. Peter knew Wade could shoot at least twice, once from each barrel, one for each—

"You don't want to do this, Wade," Peter said. "Let us go before you get into real trouble." Wade shook his head. Shawn's face looked like someone was squeezing his ears, wise guy Shawn, big mouth with nothing to say, big help.

Peter tried not to look at the police, police on the stairways, on both sides, squeezing, squeezing. "You won't have to go through this if you give me the gun," he said. Wade didn't move. He held the gun low but not low enough. "What do you want?" Peter asked. "I'll give you money. I'll give you all the money I've got on me." Out came his green cloth wallet. A stack of twenties sat in there because Riley was taking him to the mall to check out new VCRs after school. Before Peter could even count out the money for him, Wade shook his head.

"I need a ride," Wade said. "Take care of my uncle."

"I can get Riley for you," Peter said.

If the police were to shoot, Peter thought, they'd all

be dead. He and Wade and Shawn. There were police on both stairways. Crossfire. Cut down in a crossfire. If Wade didn't shoot him and Shawn, the police would. Peter remembered Sergeant Gallagher talking about hostage situations in *You And The Law*. "Seal off the area," Sergeant Gallagher said. "That's the standard operating procedure. Then you talk. You try to open communication. But if the subject makes an overt action, the police take him out."

"Shoot to wound him?" Peter had asked.

"To kill. That's the only way to be sure he won't hurt anyone else."

Eventually the cops would shoot. They wouldn't hold back forever.

"Where is Riley?" Wade said.

"Cutting school," Peter said. "He's sleeping in. The lazy bum. I can get him to come here. I'll call him." Shawn said nothing, which was okay with Peter because Shawn would probably wise off and make it worse. "Riley's supposed to meet me here soon. I'll pay him to drive you to Vermont." Peter made everything up as he went along, lies flying out of his mouth. "Let me go, and I'll get him here. I'll call him."

Wade mumbled something that sounded like, "Okay."

"I'll go in the office and use the phone," Peter said. "They'll let me because I have to call my mother sometimes."

Wade nodded his head. Peter turned to the office door.

Four steps, maybe five, and he'd be out of it. Free. Safe. One step. Second step. Stop. Turn. "Let Burns go. Let him come with me."

Wade shook his head. He raised the shotgun and pointed it at Shawn. Wade would not let his last hostage go. Wade meant business. Shawn started to shake.

Peter turned. Another step. Peter knew if Wade figured out that he had lied, Wade would shoot him. Not like in the movies. Yes, like in the movies. Gross, splatter. Just walk like you told the truth. His hand coated with sweat couldn't turn the doorknob. It wouldn't turn. Like Teflon, he thought. Teflon. Won't stick. Turn. Open. In. The office was empty. The big office was empty. Then he saw a group of secretaries down in the passageway that led to guidance. He swept his hair off his forehead. As he walked toward them, his knees tried to fall.

The secretary with the accent said, "Peter, for Christ's sake, get over here."

Like a fullback running through a hole, John rushed down the basement corridor. "That's Wade," he told the cop who grabbed his arm. "That's my friend."

"Are you sure?" the cop asked.

"There's only one Wade Rule who goes to this school," John said. "Let me go talk to him."

The cop held onto John's arm with a grip that could throw him against the row of lockers without warning.

"He's holding two kids hostage up there right now. We don't need another one."

"Wade! Wade! Wade!" The name banged off the walls and pummeled John. He thought Wade must feel each shout like a rock aimed straight at his head. "Shouting like that will drive him crazy," John told the cop. "He hates shouting."

The cop changed his grip to a friendly hold on top of John's shoulder. "Hey, Lieutenant!" he shouted. "We got a kid here who can help."

As Mr. B made the turn halfway down the stairs, Sergeant Gallagher, without moving the shotgun from its aim, held up his left palm. Then he pointed his index finger to the second floor. Mr. B retreated to the second floor corridor.

On the first floor, having walked within a hundred feet of Wade, Mr. Greenberg tried to get his attention without yelling as loudly as the cops. "Wade," he said. The boy turned.

Mr. Greenberg thought how empty this corridor was compared to the one below, where cops in uniform and cops in suits crowded, bumped, and bristled as if dancing out of time to the static crack of walkie-talkies. "Wade?" Mr. Greenberg asked. "Will you let that kid go?"

Wade faced Mr. Greenberg. "No," Wade said as quietly, as neutrally, as if he'd refused an offer of a glass of water.

"Wade!" the police yelled. "Put down the gun! Put it down!" The hall distorted their voices into hollow echoes. "Rule! Walk away! Put the gun down! Wade!"

"Wade," Mr. Greenberg said, "this is serious. You let one go; let the other one go. Then we're done." Wade was not a bad kid, not mean, not stupid, though he always looked like the troop had left him lost in the woods.

"Wade!" the police yelled. "Wade!"

"Do you know who I am?" Mr. Greenberg asked. "Do you know me?"

"Wade!" the police yelled. "Wade!"

Mr. Greenberg could see Wade's fingers inside the trigger guard, but the gun pointed down. Slowly Wade turned and nodded to Mr. Greenberg.

"Wade!" the police yelled. "Put the gun down!"

The hostage screamed, "I'm fucking scared!" Bending double as though cramps ate his stomach, he couldn't keep tears out of his wavering voice. "Why are you doing this?"

"If you want somebody, let me come up," Mr. Greenberg said. "Let him go."

With his left hand Wade patted his bandolier full of shells, as if he were pulling his suspenders with pride.

"Why me?" the hostage screamed. He stepped away from Wade. Without raising it to his shoulder, Wade swiveled the gun toward the hostage, who grabbed his gut again as if pain sliced his middle. "I'm fucking scared!"

"Don't shoot him!" Mr. Greenberg yelled.

"Wade!" the police yelled. "Put the gun down! Walk away!"

The hostage, holding his stomach, moved back to Wade. They stood just away from the doorless stairway that led to the west exit. The hostage shook and trembled. His voice whined tears. Mr. Greenberg thought the hostage was about to lose it and run or attack Wade. Either way he'd get himself shot. "Let me take his place," Mr. Greenberg said to Wade. "Look, you just got this poor schmuck off the street." He hoped that was true, that Wade hadn't picked some kid he wanted to punish.

Wade shook his head.

What could Wade want? Mr. Greenberg wondered. A cop sidled along the wall and told him to step back, closer to the bio wing in case Wade became violent. Wade could try to shoot him. Mr. Greenberg moved to the open space where the science wing T'd into the main corridor.

"What do you want?" Mr. Greenberg asked Wade. On the stairways at either side of Wade the police shouted. "What do you want?" Mr. Greenberg asked again.

Again the hostage walked toward the steps. Again Wade pointed his gun at him and then pointed it to a place on the floor, as if designating a spot for him to stand, his place of death, his grave. Mr. Greenberg felt he were watching a child get dashed down a waterfall.

"Wade!" the police shouted. "Wade!"

"Don't shoot!" Mr. Greenberg yelled. "Don't shoot

him!"

"Wade!" the police shouted.

"Let me take his place," Mr. Greenberg said.

Wade raised the gun to his shoulder and pointed it down the hallway at Mr. Greenberg who could see the eye at the other end of the barrel. Mr. Greenberg dove into the side hallway. The carpet burned his hands and face.

The shotgun in his hand reminded Wade of the perfect day when he'd shot his buck all by himself back in Newfound. His father had said, "What a beauty. You're a man now, ahead of schedule." A perfect day, he thought. I have to wait here until Riley comes, just until Riley comes, and get these people out of my way, and pick up Maria. In his pocket was Maria's napkin with the map drawn on it, the wrong map. He carried it for the chocolate syrup kiss from her lips. Peter, who never lied, had promised to get Riley. With the return address on Uncle Andrew's letter, Riley would be able to find Uncle Andrew's trailer. Riley would come here, out front. Wasn't that what he had told Peter? What had he told Peter? Goddamn it, what had he told Peter? There was all this yelling. He had a gun. He had a hostage. Couldn't they all shut up? There wasn't supposed to be all this bullshit. How could he light the world in all this confusion?

Had Wade hidden from the truth? Had he hidden inside all his lies until his luck would never hold? How could he light the world if he had to lie all the time? He didn't lie all the time, but he couldn't deny he lied often. Would he have to be accurate always, never lie, even to his mother? Did he have to lie to light the world? Did that mean he could never light the world or just that his luck wouldn't hold? When he'd shot the buck, he hadn't lied, not at all. Why had he changed?

Wade needed Shawn, and he needed for the others to leave him alone. He pointed his gun at Mr. Greenberg. It had worked before. It made them shut up. He pushed the safety forward. Every time you closed the gun after breaking it, the safety catch activated. The stock tucked into his shoulder. With internal hammers, the barrels made a smooth clean line right out into space, all the way from his eye to the emptiness of the corridor. He kept his face away from the barrel as his father had taught him. Dark as it was, he could see anything that crossed the light.

The police officer on the doorless west stairway, half a flight below the open space where Wade Rule stood, held his .38 special, fully cocked, in both hands. He kept the short barrel centered on Rule's body, though a little to the right because he tended to shoot left. At fifteen or twenty feet he had a good shot at the subject. The boy hadn't spoken. He hadn't even shown a sign he knew officers were present. Twice he'd used his shotgun to tether his hostage. The officer believed the boy had gone into the thousand yard stare. Someone at the other end of the corridor had tried to talk to the boy. Other cops had tried to get him to talk. Everyone was still trying. His finger inside the trigger guard, the boy raised the shotgun to his shoulder and pointed it at the hostage. You don't need to aim with a shotgun, the officer thought. He squeezed the trigger of the .38.

At the second floor landing Mr. B heard a hollow crack, a concussion like an air-filled paper bag popped in a closed room, a trick he'd pulled from time to time on his colleagues. This was not a trick. He backed away from the railing. He'd locked all the doors. There was no place for him to hide.

It pushed Wade back, like being punched in the stomach. "Why did you hit me?" he asked. Maria's napkin rested in his pocket. Time. Where's Riley?

On the east stairway Sergeant Gallagher sighted his shotgun through the glass panels at Wade, who was at least twenty-five feet away. He wished he could have let Mr. B talk to the boy, but the situation was past that. Elbow on knee, foot raised two stairs, he steadied his weapon. Wade raised his weapon. CRACK! A pistol shot. The kid turned, aimed at the police. Sergeant Gallagher fired. BOOM! And again. BOOM!

Blinding white pain in his head. Wade kept fingers on both triggers. A shotgun can improve your luck. But no man's luck holds; we are only time's napkin with which she wipes her lips. Wade heard a terrific explosion smash the air as his fingers in reflex pulled both triggers at once. He did not hear shoes clack on stairs, the click-clack of cops running up the stairs, to the first floor and to the landing above it.

Wade did not feel Peter's fear as the office door burst open. Peter ducked, but it was not Wade. It was Shawn. Shawn vaulted the counter by the mailboxes, jumped on the window ledge, and opened the window. "I'm out of here!" he shouted. Rushing over to the wall, Peter watched Shawn race down the hill and across the street to the store. The driveway in front of the school was filled with squad cars, dazzling blue lights, no sirens, no Riley.

As the police sealed off the entrances to the corridor, Wade did not see Mr. Greenberg walk down the hallway, rubbing his hand over his carpet burned face. The EMTs moved Wade from the floor to a stretcher. His hair made a mashed and matted halo above his oxygen-masked face. They carried him past the police and down the east stairwell. The wire-mesh window between the doors was shattered. Glass glimmered on the carpet. Wade's blood glowed dark on the carpet, not liquid, but gelatinous.

Wade

The weather changed abruptly. From a high of nearly sixty degrees, the temperature dropped into the teens that night and didn't rise above freezing the next day. Nor did Wade Rule's luck hold. He died in the hospital with a .33 caliber shotgun pellet in his brain, never having regained consciousness, never having seen any light save his own.

Wade would never know that John asked Peter why the police hadn't shot to wound him or to disarm him. He would never hear Peter tell John how dangerous it had been, how scared he was standing in the hallway with Wade holding the gun and Shawn losing all control. John focused on who shot first, Wade or the police, the issue of fairness appealing to his love of games. Peter told him that some things count, that you couldn't always take back what you'd said or done with a "just kidding."

Wade didn't sit in Mac's first period social studies class three days after the shooting, when Shawn Burns returned, walking with a cocky swagger that he exaggerated as if to deflect any wisecracks. At his seat he curled one arm over the top of the chair and one on the desk top and twisted slightly to the left, toward the windows so that he faced neither teacher nor students.

"Shawn," Mac said, and he stood away from the teacher desk that he usually leaned against, "do you want to tell us about it?"

Shawn's eyes narrowed. "Read the book," he said. Then he laughed, but he told them nothing about his experience. He never let on that he swallowed meds day and night and went to counseling twice a week.

Wade would never discover what Maria thought about him.

"You were very lucky, Maria," Rich said one day at work.

"He wasn't after me," Maria said.

"He wasn't after the two he took hostage, either," Rich said. "They were lucky to survive."

"He wasn't going to shoot anybody," Maria said.

She wasn't going to argue with this sweet man, but she refused to assign outcomes to luck because that sounded too much like her father. For Steven Blanchard, things happened because of luck, in his case usually bad. He held to a raggedy destiny that had it in for him. Maria wasn't so sure about denying that importance to Wade.

Wade had swallowed some destiny whole. He had been hungry for so long, that when he finally saw a table he could sit at, he tried to eat everything at once. Maria hadn't known that he would pursue his goals so ferociously, to get to Vermont, to help his uncle, to help her. She wasn't so sure about this last part. She'd told Sergeant Gallagher that they weren't boyfriend-girlfriend. Only after Wade's death had she figured out that he was in love with her. She'd thought of him as lonely, lonely in his hopes and plans, happy to share them with her as she was happy to share hers with him. She hadn't known his nightmares weren't just bad dreams.

Wade would never learn what his mother and father wanted. When Mr. Greenberg drove to the Rule apartment to offer his condolences, Wade's parents listened to him while blocking the doorway. Each of them stood about as tall as Wade, an eerie reminder of the dead boy. A wooden rail painted the saddest shade of gray Mr. Greenberg had ever seen made an L around the porch. At the far end of the L he stood out in the open, isolated, sounding his sorrow while Velma and Frank Rule stood shoulder to shoulder. As he turned to leave, Wade's mother asked him if he knew whether they'd found her key.

"Key?" he asked.

"My house key," she said. "I'm sure Wade had it with him. I've asked the police to return it, but they just give me the run around."

The father had asked the police for the return of Wade's shotgun. "My brother gave him that gun," he said. "It was always a good gun. Both of us always liked that gun."

"Highly unusual," Sergeant Gallagher told Mr. Greenberg when he inquired about the shotgun and the house key. "In cases like this or suicides, the family almost never wants the weapon returned. And we never did find the house key. Maybe Wade wasn't planning on going back. Lucky thing for them."

Mr. Greenberg didn't visit Wade's parents again. Nor did he call to report his failure to find the key. He had thought about it until he phoned the funeral home to ask about the arrangements. He planned to make an announcement over the school's p.a. for those students who wanted to attend the funeral or memorial service or graveside or whatever they were having. The undertaker said there were no arrangements. Wade was cremated; his parents came one night for his ashes and carried them off in the dark.

Acknowledgments

My thanks to the following writers and critical readers for their suggestions, encouragement, and comradeship hiking in the writing neck of the woods: Katherine Towler, John Cawelti, Jane Hunt, Tricia Bauer, Peter Roth, Don Stanger, Rick Carey, Mark Roth, Sean Connell, Ben Schwartz, Tim Deal, Jon Greenberg, George Kelly, Dana Biscotti Myskowski, Bob Begiebing, Don Gemberling, Bill Bozzone, Dave Ellis, Wesley McNair, Bob Hutter, Rob Greene, Darren Cormier, Derrick Craigie, Randy Dunham, Connie Rosemont, Rich Morena, and Alan Lindsay.

Special thanks to Jack Scovil, my late agent, who always believed in Wade's story.

And to my wife, Teresa Ceballos, love of mine.

About the Author

A native of Northern New England, Merle Drown has written stories, essays, plays, reviews, and two novels, *Plowing Up a Snake* and *The Suburbs of Heaven*. He has received fellowships from the National Endowment for the Arts and the New Hampshire Arts Council and teaches in Southern New Hampshire University's M.F.A. program. The father of three sons, he lives with his wife Teresa Ceballos in Concord, New Hampshire, and Toronto.

CPSIA information can be obtained at www.ICGtesting.com
Printed in the USA
LVOW08s1642110815

449697LV00001B/87/P